The Amulets

Book One of
The Amulets Trilogy

J. Lawson

Dri,
Much love and
appreciation for
all your support.
Stay magical,
friend ♡

Lawson

Dedication

This book is dedicated in a big way to my best friend, Laura. Through the course of twenty-one years of friendship, she has done nothing but support me and the idea that I could complete a book. When a spark of an idea lead to a four-hour coffee klatch, it appeared the time had finally come to give it a shot and this is the outcome; book one of a trilogy. She has spent countless hours providing support, review, and talking me through blocks. You're a rock star, bestie! I couldn't have done this without you.

Contents

Chapter One – Transformation
Chapter Two – Tentative Friendship
Chapter Three – The New Guy
Chapter Four – The Reset
Chapter Five – Secret Revealed
Chapter Six – History
Chapter Seven – Normal
Chapter Eight – The Date
Chapter Nine – A Sadness
Chapter Ten – In Memoriam
Chapter Eleven – Bedtime Stories
Chapter Twelve – Unease
Chapter Thirteen – Secret Exposed
Chapter Fourteen – Explanation
Chapter Fifteen – Victoria's Revelation
Chapter Sixteen – Auggie's Warning
Chapter Seventeen – Victoria's Story
Chapter Eighteen – Rescue Attempt
Chapter Nineteen – Sacrifice
Chapter Twenty – A New War
Chapter Twenty-One – Aftermath

Chapter One
Transformation

"Just stack the new shipment in the back! With the new store layout happening tomorrow night, it doesn't make any sense to shelve them just to have to move them again." Ryan called from his desk through the open door of his office. "I don't understand why the sudden increase in demand for fantasy books," he muttered quietly. "It's just catering to the dreamers who contribute nothing more to society than wild discussions on topics that have no relevance to anything in the real world. We need less dreamers and more concrete intellects." He got up and walked to the door of his office. "Jordan! Are you listening to me?"

Jordan Maren was leaning against a large pallet in the stock room of Shamore Book Store, engrossed in the jacket of one of the new arrival books. Finally, a fantasy novel that wasn't about witches or werewolves, she thought to herself. She understood the draw of those kinds of books to the general public, but there was nothing "general" about Jordan. The whole concept of "people turning into creatures" was one she had had quite enough of in her life, and reading about it simply didn't interest her. She finished the jacket of the book about a fictional land with royal families, dragons, and magic, and held it to her chest. She lifted her eyes to the rest of the stacks of books on the pallet, but did not focus on them. Her mind drifted as she took stock of her life thus far.

From a young age, Jordan had been keeping something from everyone else in the tiny town of Shamore, Vermont.

Now, at the age of twenty-two, her friends, parents, and the entire community still knew nothing of her biggest secret. When she had turned eight years old, her mother and father had finally allowed her to play in the woods that butted up to her back yard and ran along the edge of town. They made her promise to stay only on the trails so she wouldn't get lost or hurt, and she had done this for a short time, but the dense trees and crumbling logs with their allure and look of adventure had been too much for her wild heart to resist. She soon started taking the path from her backyard through the woods until she was deep enough she knew she would be out of sight of anyone and then she would take off in any random direction to explore the thicker parts of the woods where the trails did not lead. Gradually, as her familiarity with the woods grew, the time she spent out in the woods lengthened as did the distance to which she travelled.

It was on one of these longer walks, in the heat of a June afternoon shortly after she turned ten, that she first pushed her way through some rather thick brush and came upon a clearing that held a beautiful pond nestled in amongst some mossy rocks and weeping willow curtains. From then on, she spent many afternoons there, lazing by the water, enjoying the cooler breeze that would occasionally play across the, somehow always still, surface of the water. Jordan had marveled at how, even though it looked like the area around it hadn't been touched in ages, the water seemed so clean and the surrounding banks were so inviting. At times, it was almost as if she could see all the way to the bottom near the middle of the pond.

One particularly warm day, the heat and lack of the comforting breeze she occasionally enjoyed was too much for her to bear. She removed her socks and shoes and gently dipped her feet and legs into the cool water. Immediately, she felt a cooling feeling, not only to her feet and legs, but one that seemed to radiate into her very core. She squeezed her fingers into the grass of the bank she was sitting on, closed her eyes, let her head fall back, and breathed deeply through her nose. After a few minutes, she opened her eyes and stared at the canopy of leaves far above her head. The cooling feeling in her core was gone and she swished her feet gently in the water as she stared above her. She noticed birds and even some bugs flying around far above. She squinted and thought it seemed odd; the flying insects seemed to be almost too small and far away to be possible to see. She didn't remember ever having seen insects that high in the trees before, but she figured she just hadn't been paying attention. Her eyes followed a yellow-winged bird as it flitted back and forth between two branches and she suddenly noticed she wasn't only watching the wings beating; she could *hear* them beating. But how could that be? The bird was barely close enough to see. How could she hear something so subtle? She shook her head and looked back out over the water. A soft rustling sound to her left caught her attention and she turned her head to see a fox creeping to the edge of the pond and pausing before dipping its head to lap at the water. Jordan took another deep breath and caught a whiff of something she couldn't quite put her finger on. It reminded her of the smell of her pet dog, Rex, who had passed a couple years ago, but just slightly different. Was she smelling the fox? She smiled to herself and lifted her feet from the pond, pulling her knees to her chest. She had to be imagining these feeling of her senses being so incredibly heightened. Maybe it was just the calm quietness of the forest or the relief of the pond cooling her that made her more receptive to these things.

She reached over and put her socks and shoes back on. As she rose and brushed dirt and grass from the seat of her pants, the fox startled and ran swiftly into the trees. Jordan didn't think she had been so loud as to scare the fox from so far away, but she shrugged and turned back in the direction she would take back to her house. The smell and the sight of the bear hit her at the same time and her heart skipped a few beats as their eyes met. The bear was maybe ten feet away and, even at a distance, she could see it was enormous. It had to be at least two-hundred pounds and looked angry someone had decided to visit the pond at the same time it had. Jordan's heart began beating again rapidly and she felt herself start to shake. Through her cloud of terror, she noticed she wasn't shaking as much as she was… vibrating. She chanced a look away from the bear and glanced down at her arms and legs. Her eyes grew wide as she saw they were beginning to darken and bend at odd angles. She felt the same cooling feeling throughout her body that she had when she first put her feet into the pond. As she looked back at the bear, it seemed to get even taller. In fact, everything around her seemed to be getting taller. As she began to panic, the bear seemed to also decide the situation wasn't quite right and, to her relief, it turned and retreated through the forest. She could still hear it long after she was unable to see it and it wasn't until the sound faded from her ears that she felt confident to look back at herself. What she saw almost made her faint.

She thought she had to be hallucinating. She had been wearing a red tank top and blue jean shorts when she entered the woods and her tan legs had ended in white socks with light blue sneakers. All she was seeing now, however, were thin, grey-haired legs. *FOUR* thin, grey-haired legs. She tried to back away from what she was seeing, but her extra pair of legs threw off her muscle memory for walking and she tumbled backward. As she rolled to the side, she saw something fluffy whip by in her peripheral line of vision and realized there was a long, thick tail attached to her hind end. This can't be happening, she remembered thinking to herself. She figured she must have fallen asleep in the heat and this was a dream; she was dreaming she turned into a dog. It would have been a nice dream, except she had a level of awareness that, if this was a dream, she needed to wake from it soon since she needed to get back home before her parents began to worry about her. She slowly got up and took a few moments to get her coordination together in order to make her way back over to the bank of the pond. The only creature around now was a beautiful white swan on the opposite side of the pond by the curtain of willow branches. It floated silently on the water and she couldn't be bothered by its presence in her frantic mental state. She looked into the water and her reflection took her breath away. She wasn't a dog as she had originally thought. She was much bigger than a dog. She was a wolf! As she stood staring at her reflection, her thoughts returned to the confusion she had felt at her heightened senses from earlier that afternoon. She supposed the sharper vision, hearing, and smell made sense now, but it also didn't make sense. She had been a human girl at that point. Was she dreaming those sensory increases? Why would those senses have come to her before she became a wolf? And *how* did she become a wolf? She shook her head again. It felt like she'd been doing that a lot in this particular visit to the woods. What was she thinking? She hadn't become a wolf. This was a dream. It didn't matter when the dream had started; it mattered that it *was* a dream and she needed to wake up.

She sat back on her haunches and thought. She had always been astute from a very young age and, while most kids her age would have been in a blind panic, she knew she needed to think clearly. How could she get herself to wake up? She took a deep breath and yelled "Wake up!" What came out was a sharp, high pitched combination of a yip and a bark. She managed to startle herself, the swan in the pond flapped its wings in alarm, and a number of birds took flight at the sound, but she still had four legs and fur, so she thought some more. She no longer had opposable thumbs, so she couldn't pinch herself like she had seen in movies. She looked around and noticed a thick, broken branch on a bush to her right. She rose and slowly made her way over to the bush. She was starting to figure out the routine of walking with an extra set of legs. When she reached the broken branch, she rocked back and then leaned hard toward the bush, letting the branch dig into her right hind leg. "Ow!" she cried, but what came out was a shrieking yelp like that of a wounded dog. She was starting to feel the panic rise again. The loud noise hadn't woken her. The sharp pain hadn't woken her. She was running out of ideas as well as time. The sun was dipping lower, which was evident by the darkening in the woods. What was she going to do, she wondered? Should she just sit and wait for her parents to worry enough to come looking for her? Should she start walking home and hope she woke somewhere on the way?

She laid down on the forest floor and thought some more. Could it possibly be that this wasn't a dream? She had been reading books about this kind of thing ever since she had learned to read, but those books weren't real and these things didn't happen in real life. What was going on right now in the clearing only happened in fairy tales and fantasy books. Yet, she had tried everything she could think of to bring herself out of a dream, and that hadn't worked either. She may have to consider the fact that reality might not be all she had been told it was and this craziness could be a part of her new reality.

Being the logical kid she was and drawing from the down-to-earth nature of her parents, she knew that, as terrified and confused as she was, there was nothing to be achieved by panicking, even though she wanted to. She had to calm down and think. She rested her head on her paws and sighed heavily. As she watched the light through the branches grow dimmer, once again the cooling feeling washed through her body. Her muscles stiffened and she lifted her head again to look around. As she went to push her paw forward, she noticed it was no longer a paw, but a human hand once again. She looked down and saw the red tank top and blue jean shorts as well. Gingerly, she put her human muscle memory to work again and slowly stood. She was back to normal as far as she could tell. She sighed an enormous sigh of relief and walked over to the pond to look in one last time. Yes, she was back to herself again. With a quick glance back to the woods where she had seen the fox and the bear, she pushed back through the dense brush toward the path that would lead her back to her house. The swan seemed to watch her as she left the clearing, then turned and swam away from Jordan's retreating steps. She knew she should have been jogging, but her mind was reeling with what had happened. Or, maybe what she had dreamed happened? She still couldn't believe it had been real, but she knew she didn't feel like she had just woken up either. She had felt very present and aware the entire time everything had been happening. She shook her head one more time and picked up the pace as she reached the trail that would lead her home.

That had been Jordan's first transformation, but it certainly hadn't been her last. She had thought on it obsessively afterward and considering the circumstances of that day, she finally worked out that the stress and fear of seeing the bear had triggered the transformation and the relaxing had enabled her to will herself to change back. With many visits back to the pond and much practice, after a few months she had been able to initiate the change and return on her own with no external stimulus. Being able to control the transformations had made her feel better, but even now, twelve years later, she was no closer to understanding *why* she was able to do what she could do. She thought many times of asking her parents about it, but she feared her parents would think she was crazy and send her to a psychologist or, worse, some other kind of doctor for medical testing. She decided no one could know about her abilities and had spent the years keeping her secret from everyone she knew. Only during her alone time in the woods did she allow herself to acknowledge the change and she even began to enjoy her time as a wolf. She loved how fast she was and her endurance. In fact, the time she spent running through the woods for hours seemed to increase her stamina in her human form as well. Her muscles in her arms and legs had developed significantly over the years, and the constant exercise kept her lean. These features combined with her long, dark brown hair and light blue eyes meant she was attractive enough to escape attention in the form of ridicule from any cruel peers. She had also become decent at sports and would have likely been good at basketball given she was fairly tall for a girl, but she maintained her distance by only participating in track and field sports which were much more individual based and allowed her to not have to participate closely with any team and, more importantly to her, any specific people. She had made it to graduation flying pretty well under the radar.

Because, as much as she enjoyed her ability at times, she still felt like a bit of an outsider, unable to share this significant aspect of her life with anyone. She purposely avoided getting too close to anyone, even after graduation, for fear of some event causing a spontaneous change like her first transformation in the woods all those years ago. This solitary tendency of hers resulted in her spending most of the time she wasn't at school or in the woods engrossed in her books. She loved to read about faraway places and magic. Fantasy books were her favorite because they provided her an escape, but she still couldn't stand to read about humans turning to creatures. To everyone else, those were just stories based on nothing other than legends and myths, and the people who read them thought of them as entertainment and something to fantasize about being able to do. But Jordan was living that world and knew how unexciting and lonesome it could really be. The falsity of it irked her; even made her a little angry at times. She had started working at the bookstore almost six years ago as a way to have easy access to her favorite hobby, but it had come with the added expense of having to talk to people about their love of these ridiculous human/creature books.

Still, she thought, coming out of her daydream, it was worth it to find books like the one against her chest. She couldn't wait until it was in the system so she could purchase it and read it by her pond in the woods with the swan who so often kept her company from the opposite side.

"Jordan," yelled a voice right behind her and she jumped, dropping the book, and spinning around to face Ryan who had come into the stockroom and had clearly seen her staring off into space.

"God, Ryan, you scared me!" Jordan said, her hand on her heart and the other digging her nails into her leg to help her redirect her focus from the cooling feeling that was beginning in her core. This always happened when she got startled, upset, or very angry. An elevation in heart rate due to an emotional stimulus was exactly what she tried to avoid in hopes of staving off an involuntary transformation. Pain, she had found, was a good distraction, and even now, the cooling feeling stopped in her limbs and spread no farther. She took a few deep breaths, still looking at Ryan.

"I'm sorry, but I've been calling for you for five minutes," Ryan said, a little less angrily. "There are five customers in the store and you're the only one here until 4:00pm when the new girl starts." He picked up the book Jordan had dropped and looked at the cover. "Oh, geez," he said, rolling his eyes and handing the book back to her. "More fantasy novels. See what I mean? People who read these things are so dreamy and distracted. Who knows how long you would've been back here if I hadn't come and found you? Why can't you read something concrete? Or educational? Or *real*?!"

"It's just part of my charm," Jordan smiled. "Plus, my knowing about 'these things' has helped your sales. You had almost no fantasy section before I started here and now look! You're doing an entirely new layout to accommodate a new, huge fantasy section *and* your sales have increased by twenty percent, mostly due to the younger crowd in town buying 'these things'. So, stop being such a crab and embrace it!"

"I still can't believe we are having to cut the travel section in half, but the business section too? It kills me," he said, turning to walk back to the stockroom door.

"Oh, please, Ryan," Jordan said exasperatedly. "Travel? No one in this town *goes* anywhere! The people in this town have been here for generations. No one moves. No one travels. Most of them don't even go on vacation! And as far as business, more than half of the people over eighteen work at the old mill or the annex near the ravine. There isn't exactly a strong entrepreneurial drive in this town. The business books and travel books were collecting dust. The shelves were disgusting when we cleaned them off. And most of them weren't even published in this decade. This reset is going to make so much more sense, you'll see." She stacked the book back on top of the pile of others with the same title and hustled out of the stockroom behind Ryan and back to the sales floor to help the customers.

At 3:30pm, Jordan went back to Ryan's office. The customers had cleared out and the store was temporarily empty. Things would pick up again in about two to three hours when people were home from work and school and when supper had been eaten. Jordan leaned against the door frame and watched Ryan work at his computer he always kept on a counter at the back of his office against the wall, his back to the door. His regular desk sat in the middle of the room with papers piled all over it and a single, tiny clear spot in the middle where she saw him eat his lunch on occasion. She had known Ryan for years; since she started shopping in the book store at a young age. He was in his early forties but looked much younger. He took care of himself and his just-under-six-feet frame was trim. His dark auburn hair was kept short at the sides with a fade cut to longer, messy hair on top of his head and his hazel eyes looked intelligent behind black framed glasses. He had always been a cranky kind of guy, but his curtness and apparent lack of ability to smile had never bothered her. He had been able to show her the books she was looking for and, after a while, she stared to share with him what she knew about the genres he was less familiar with. Sometimes he even seemed to listen to her, albeit halfheartedly. When she turned sixteen, he had offered her a job in his store. She had been surprised because he always frowned on her reading choices, but she gladly accepted knowing she would get a discount on her beloved books, as well as order in the ones she wanted. And even though she hated talking to people about their silly fairy tale obsessions, talking about books, even crummy ones, was still better than talking about almost anything else.

"Hey, boss," she said to his back. She saw him jump and heard him curse under his breath.

"How many times have I told you not to sneak up on me like that?" he asked, spinning his chair around to face her. "You're going to give me a heart attack and if I die, you're out of a job."

"Well, you scared the crap out of me earlier, so we're even," she laughed, walking to his desk and lifting herself to sit in the small clear spot. "And if you don't want people to sneak up on you, put your computer on this desk and face your door. If a robber came in while you were alone, you'd never see them coming facing the back wall."

"If I had my computer on this desk then where would you plant your ass?" he said, grabbing the side of her jeans and tugging until she shifted her weight off his desk. "I can't have my computer on this desk. If I face the door, there are too many distractions. I need to be able to focus. And before you say anything," he rushed on as she opened her mouth to comment on his last statement, "I can't shut the door because then I can't hear the bell and don't know if anyone's in the store."

"If there's someone in the store, your associate should be taking care of them, right? That *is* why you hired me, isn't it?"

"It is," he agreed. "And we saw how well you were taking care of those five customers in the store earlier today while you were in the back room having a fifteen-minute daydream. What do you want?"

"Tell me about this new girl starting today. What did you say her name was? It didn't sound familiar when you told me before and I know almost everyone in this town."

"Her name is Georgia Linden and you wouldn't know her because she's not from here. She and her mom just moved to town. They lived in a small town in New Hampshire, but they relocated here. Actually, I think her mom was originally from here or something," he shrugged, turning his chair back to his computer. "Doesn't really matter to me. She has a decent knowledge of books and she's new here so she's got open availability. That's really all I'm looking for. Now go do what I pay you for and let me know when she gets here."

Jordan walked back to the door. "I thought that's what the bell was for," she tossed over her shoulder, and then hustled back out to the sales floor. Ryan was a fairly relaxed guy, but you could only push him so far and she figured she had almost reached her quota. Back behind the register again, she leaned back against the counter and crossed her arms; her "thinking pose" her mom had always called it.

The new girl, Georgia, was from out of town. She thought for a while but couldn't remember a time when someone had moved to Shamore from somewhere else. And in her entire memory, she could only think of two people who had ever moved out of it. One had to go take care of family and the other had joined the peace corps and then ended up staying. The kids at school had often joked that the only way out of this town was as ashes on the wind. Death was an escape from life maybe, but even buried, you'd be stuck here forever. It might have been morbid, but it was true. From what Ryan said, it sounded like her mom had been one of the lucky *very* few to have escaped the town. Why in the world would she want to come back?

Jordan didn't hate Shamore, but it was pretty one-dimensional. Nothing ever happened here and it was stuck somewhat in the past. Being so far away from any major city, nothing ever happened in their town. There was nothing unique or outstanding about the town, so it didn't draw in any tourists. The vast expanse of forest for miles in multiple directions combined with the series of ravines made it impossible to get a cell or wireless internet signal, and most families hadn't even moved past the rotary dial phones on their walls, much less cell phones and laptop computers. The few who did have them complained constantly of the lack of service and spotty connectivity. There wasn't even a cable TV provider that felt it worth the expense to provide service to the town.

Due to the lack of diversity in the job sector and the distance between Shamore and the closest neighboring towns, no one seemed to have much of a drive to further their education past high school. Most kids did graduate, and the boys got jobs at the mill, despite what their aptitudes had been in school. Those not suited for or interested in mill work would work at the grocer, the bank, the police station, or doing construction or other similar jobs. The girls often worked at the shops in town, the hair dresser's, restaurants, doing cleaning, or at any of the other handful of odd jobs around town. People got married at the chapel and then moved in to one of the few houses that happened to be empty at the time. The houses were all old, but almost all were well maintained and had been remodeled as time had gone by. Occasionally, someone from one of the old families would build a new house on the edge of the woods, but it didn't happen often.

Jordan uncrossed her arms and pulled the book she had been reading that week out from under the counter. She preferred not to get too close to anyone, what with the massive secret she was trying to keep, and she wasn't looking to make a bosom friend, but she couldn't deny this Georgia girl and her mother intrigued her. Maybe she'd put a little effort into being friendly to draw out some info about the world outside of Shamore. She smiled to herself. The new girl couldn't possibly be any weirder than her, anyway. Right?

Chapter Two
Tentative Friendship

The bell above the door to the bookstore tinkled and Jordan looked up from the copy of "The Thorn and the Stone." She liked to read when there was down time at the store and no side work to be done. A tall girl with dirty blonde, waist-length hair walked in and shut the door behind her.

She walked up to the desk and smiled shyly at Jordan. "Hi," she said, putting out her hand in greeting. "My name is Georgia Linden. I'm supposed to have my first training shift today. I was told to ask for Ryan."

Jordan extended her hand as well and shook Georgia's. A familiar cooling sensation appeared in her hand for a brief second giving her a moment of alarm before it disappeared just as quickly. Letting go of Georgia's hand, Jordan forced a smile over the confusion the cooling feeling has caused. The girl in front of her was hardly something to be scared of or upset about. Georgia's green eyes were bright and friendly. She was a few inches shorter than Jordan, which put her around five feet six inches, and they were similar lean builds. Georgia's skin was a bit fairer than Jordan's and her nose and cheekbones were dotted with a smattering of freckles. Jordan was actually looking forward to having a coworker, especially when it came to the holidays. Maybe Georgia's hand had just been cold, she thought, pushing the cooling feeling from her mind and opening her mouth to speak.

"Hey, Georgia. I'm Jordan. Ryan's in the back and I can take you to him if you're sure that's what you really want to do." She said this in a joking manner so as not to scare the poor girl on her first day.

Georgia laughed and followed as Jordan exited from behind the counter and began walking to the back of the store. "He was definitely a character when I talked to him for my interview. It was only over the phone, so I didn't know if the tone matched the mannerisms." Jordan looked over her shoulder and grimaced slightly. Georgia grinned and nodded. "I kinda figured. But I don't mind either way. I'm just excited to have gotten the job! Moving somewhere new for the first time in my life is hard but being surrounded by books will help a lot! I love the escape, especially into other times and places; King Arthur and Merlin, Lord of the Rings, Eragon, Game of Thrones, Star Trek, Star Wars... all of it. I live for books that take me somewhere else." She saw Jordan looking at her and blushed slightly. "Sorry. I could talk about books for ages. It's not like where I'm from is so bad or anything. Sometimes it's just... nice to get away."

Jordan stopped outside of Ryan's door. "I absolutely understand what you mean," she said knowingly. "And you won't find a whole lot else to keep your mind occupied in this town other than the books. I was just thinking to myself earlier I can't imagine someone wanting to move to this town, but Ryan said something earlier about your mom being from here. I guess Thomas Wolfe didn't know what he was talking about, huh?"

Georgia's smile faltered for the briefest of moments and she nodded. "Yeah. It turns out you *can* go home again."

Jordan laughed. "Hey, nice! I didn't know if you'd get the reference. Seems like you read more than fantasy. I think you and I will get along just fine." She knocked on the door frame of Ryan's office. "Fresh meat, boss," she said, nudging Georgia's shoulder with her knuckles. "I'll talk to you later. Go easy on her!" she called over her shoulder as she walked back to the sales floor. Everything Georgia had mentioned had been fantasy, but not one of them had morphing creatures. In fact, almost all of them were her favorites as well. She may not be in the market for a best friend, but Georgia should at least make life in this town a little more interesting.

Jordan looked to the door as the bell tinkled again and Mrs. Sussman, the school librarian, came in with a list in her hand. She smiled and held the list up to Jordan who waved at her and walked to the counter to do what she knew would be the yearly book order for the school library. It was the same old thing every year, Jordan thought as she searched and ordered the titles while Mrs. Sussman went on about how wild kids were these days, how books used to last for years when she was a girl and now she was lucky if they lasted through the school year, but maybe, just maybe, this year would be a little different.

Jordan had just finished Mrs. Sussman's order when Ryan and Georgia appeared at the counter. "So, that's your paperwork and safety training. I'm now putting you in Jordan's hands to show you where everything is and how to run the register. May god have mercy on your soul," he said, rolling his eyes toward the ceiling. Jordan gave a loud tsk sound. "When you're familiar with the basics, we'll get you up to speed on ordering and shipments. We're a fairly small store, so we keep it basic." He put his hand on

Georgia's shoulder briefly, then removed it as though the gesture was beyond his level of comfort. "You'll do fine here. Jordan may be a dreamer, sarcastic, and have a little more attitude than I care for…"

"Gee, boss, I didn't know you cared!" Jordan cut in with a look of mild incredulity.

"*But*," he continued, "she does know what she's doing. For whatever reason, the customers like her and she knows the ins and outs of all aspects of the business. As a matter of fact, we're changing the layout of the store in a couple days because she's found a way to peddle garbage fantasy novels like they're gold."

"Well, now you're just making me blush," Jordan said, exasperated. "Go back to your office, Ryan, before you give me a big head."

"God knows you don't need that getting any bigger," Ryan muttered, turning and walking back down the hall toward his office. "Good luck, Georgia."

"Our fearless leader," Jordan said sarcastically. "How was orientation? Did you learn how to be safe around books? No lighting matches, burning candles, or bringing gasoline into the place?"

"Oh, yes, and the theft prevention was riveting. Follow around anyone with a backpack or purse large enough to fit a book in. Oh, and watch all young people like a hawk because, you know, they all steal."

"Yep, that's it! Now on to the most important part of the job; the tour." Jordan began walking the perimeter of the store, pointing out the sections and discussing how they were categorized. "Currently we have sort of a wagon wheel layout with all of the sections running like spokes to the middle of the store where the checkout's located. It's a good system because we can see pretty much every section and it's easy to keep an eye on things and those pesky thieving young people. We won't be changing the physical layout with the change Ryan mentioned, but a few of the sections are going to get significantly culled down and the fantasy section is going to more than double."

"That sounds great! Did you really find a way to peddle fantasy like it's gold?" she asked laughing.

"Garbage fantasy, you mean? Well, I don't know about that. It was basically just giving people what they want. Ryan is dead set against fantasy having anything to offer humanity. He'd stick to travel, business, history, true crime, and text book type books exclusively if he could make a living on it. But I decided to show him what would happen if we gave the people what we wanted. There's a pretty large teen crowd in town these days. Not a lot to do around here except make babies apparently. And, even though this town is woefully behind the times, those kids *do* like the fantasy. So when he gave me control over the ordering, signage, and marketing, I showed him just what kind of business we could do. He couldn't argue with the results."

"Sounds like you have a real knack for this! You must really know how to read people and what they want."

"That's nice of you to say, but I have to be honest; it started out fairly self-serving," she chuckled. "I love the genre and I was running out of things I wanted to read. So, I started by checking out the best seller lists we get mailed to us and that Ryan has always ignored, ordered those in, and then kind of branched out from there. The rest is history," she said, stopping in front of the travel section where half of the shelves were empty.

"Is this where the expansion's happening?" asked Georgia, running her fingers along the spines of the remaining books. As she read each obscure title, the crease in her brow deepened.

"That it is. Travel and business are getting cut in half and fantasy will be expanding into the free space. We'll keep the books we're pulling off the shelves in stock for a while in case anyone wants them." At this, Jordan rolled her eyes slightly and Georgia giggled. "Then, when Ryan's convinced no one wants them and I whine enough about needing the space for additional stock that *will* sell, we'll send them back to get a partial refund and use that money to order…"

"More garbage!" Georgia finished and they both laughed.

"Oh, great," Ryan said, walking up behind them. "You're already brainwashing her." He shook his head and pulled on his blazer. "I'm going to grab supper and pick up some stuff on the way back." He said the last sentence a little tensely and Jordan looked at him questioningly. He sighed. "Our supply shipment never came this week and we need paper towels and toilet paper to get us through until whenever they decide to bring us our stock. Is no one reliable anymore? It's not like we're trying to run a business here or anything. Anyway, I'll be back before closing to count drawers and you girls can cut out a little early. Jordan, you'll be here long enough hours the next few nights getting everything shifted and switched around."

"I'm more than willing to help, too," Georgia said. "That way it won't make Jordan's nights as long and I'll learn where everything goes much faster if I help put away new stock and even by pulling the old stuff."

"Sounds like a great plan to me," Jordan said, looking to Ryan. He nodded.

"I'm fine with it if you are. I know this reset is your 'baby'." He gave one of his rare half smiles and pulled the door open. "See you girls later."

"That's a bummer about the delivery not coming," Georgia said sympathetically.

"Yeah, it's probably just some new guy on the delivery route that doesn't know the schedule yet. Or at least doesn't know what Ryan's like when he's inconvenienced. He'll learn that pretty quick." They both laughed. "Anyway, that's the tour. Come on back to the counter and I'll show you how to work the register and how to do searches in the system for the books customers want, both in stock and not. Generally, even though we have hard wire internet, there's still such a bad connection due to our beautiful landscape that we can't get the orders to go through right away and have to keep trying. So, we have to take the customers' information and try on our down time until it finally goes through, which it always does *eventually*. Oh," she said, stopping short in front of the current fantasy section and gesturing toward the shelves. "And you'll want to grab a book to read when things get slow. Job perk," she winked and Georgia beamed at her. Once she had her book, she rejoined Jordan at the counter. "So, what's your poison?" Jordan asked and Georgia held up the book. "You're kidding!" Jordan exclaimed, pulling her book from under the counter. Both girls held copies of "The Thorn and the Stone."

"Looks like we're going to get along just fine," Georgia laughed.

"I think you might be right," Jordan said. "It'll be interesting to see what it's like to have a friend." She blushed immediately after she said it, feeling suddenly very juvenile, like a kid in preschool asking another kid to be friends the first time they meet. She was usually so guarded with her thoughts and feelings; she wasn't exactly sure why she'd let that comment slip out. Just as she feared, Georgia follow up with a question.

"What do you mean?" Georgia asked. "You've lived here your whole life, haven't you? How is it possible you've not made any friends? You've been really nice to me and Ryan said people seem to like you, so did you just *choose* to not make friends? It doesn't seem likely you couldn't make them if you wanted to."

"Well," Jordan hesitated. She didn't want to let too much slip out again. "I just tend to keep more to myself when I'm not at work. I don't like sharing too much of my personal life with other people. It's just how I've always been; more private. I don't really tend to get too close to people usually."

Georgia nodded. "I can understand that. I'm the same way for the most part. It's one of the reasons I didn't mind moving here. I graduated and didn't have any real friends I was leaving behind back home, so relocating wasn't a big deal. Our town was even smaller than this one, so there weren't a whole lot of people there in the first place. We didn't even have a bookstore." Jordan looked at her sympathetically. "I know, right? It was a bummer. Anyway, I won't make you talk about yourself if you don't want to. I'm fine just talking about how amazing fantasy books are… really loudly… when Ryan's around."

Jordan couldn't help herself and burst out laughing at that comment. Georgia joined in. "You've got a deal," Jordan said when she had regained some composure. "And, maybe we can talk about ourselves a *little* now and then. I guess it's good to branch out sometimes."

"Sure, whatever you want. So, how do you run this contraption?" Georgia asked, shifting in front of the cash register.

Chapter Three
The New Guy

Ten minutes before closing, Ryan returned and pulled the drawer. "Go on and head home you two. I've got this. I'll see you both tomorrow."

The girls pulled on their hoodies and shut the door to the book store behind them.

"So, I never asked, where in town did you end up moving?" Jordan asked, leaning against the glass that made up most of the front of the store.

"My mom and I are over on Moss; the last house heading out of town."

"No way! We're practically neighbors! My parents and I live in the house on the edge of the woods two blocks over from you on Cobblestone."

"Great! Maybe we can carpool or something now and then."

"Absolutely," Jordan nodded. "Are you heading home now?"

"I don't know. It's still kind of early, but I didn't have anything else planned. Why?"

"Are you a coffee drinker? I know it's late, but there is a great makeshift café that just opened up in the grocer next door that's open for another two hours. Coffee is my life outside of books and I've been wanting to check it out since I heard about it. People have said it's really great."

"I love coffee, too. I even ordered mine in from out of town when we lived back home because I'm such a snob about it. I'd love to try new coffee."

"Great!" Jordan pushed off of the wall and they both walked next door to the grocer. When they entered, Georgia followed Jordan to the back corner of the building where the smell of ground coffee beans greeted their noses. "Isn't it just the best smell ever?"

"It absolutely is. And it smells like it is going to taste great. I hope people haven't misrepresented."

They walked up to the counter and waited. No one was there, so they rang the bell sitting next to the register.

"Hang on a sec, sorry!" a voice called from a back room, followed by a loud crash.

"Hey, is everything ok back there?" Jordan called, making her way to the swinging door of the counter. "Do you need help with anything."

A boy emerged from the back room brushing what looked like cocoa powder off one shoulder. He was tall, over six feet, and had black hair that was long enough it fell into his eyes slightly, but not enough to obscure the fact that they were a deep, dark brown, even darker than the cocoa powder he was brushing off himself. He was thin, but his muscles were well defined and he was very tan, like he was outside often. He smiled sheepishly. "No, thanks though. I

27

was trying to organize the stockroom and the shelf with our bags of chocolate powder decided to break. I saved most of them, but this one got me. It's fine though. I've smelled like much worse than cocoa before, so I'm pretty sure I'll live." He stepped behind the register and smiled fully at them this time. "So, what can I get you ladies this evening?"

"I was going to get a mocha latte, but I feel like that might be rubbing salt in your wounds," Jordan laughed. "How about a medium caramel latte? Decaf, please. I really want coffee, but I also really want to sleep tonight."

"For sure," Georgia agreed. "We're going to be up late the next few nights doing the reset. We might as well get the sleep when we can. Can I get a medium vanilla latte, please; also decaf?"

"Absolutely," the boy said, pulling the cups and starting to prepare their drinks. "So, what kind of a reset are you doing? Hopefully it's easier than the mess I'm working with back there." he asked, jerking his head back toward the room he had emerged from earlier.

"Well, I don't know if it'll be easier, but I feel like it'll be less messy, anyway," Georgia laughed.

"Yeah, we work at the bookstore next door. So, less food-related catastrophes, but it's an organizational nightmare. That and straightening out the inventory will be interesting, but I think we we're up for the job." Jordan said, nudging Georgia in a friendly way with her elbow. "We may be coming in here fairly often for a jolt to keep us going, though. My name's Jordan, by the way, and this is Georgia." Georgia gave him a wave.

"Sawyer," the boy said. "You work at the bookstore, eh? That's great to hear. I've been wanting to go in there for a while, but I haven't really had the chance yet. Plus, I was honestly kind of nervous to try it since this is such a small town and I figured the stock might reflect the generally limited interests of the residents. Are you going to do me a huge favor and tell me I'm wrong?" he grinned at them questioningly.

"Actually, if you wait a couple of days, you will be coming at the perfect time," Georgia said. "Jordan got the boss man to agree to a reset which is going to get rid of a lot of the boring and useless stuff and bring in a lot more exciting stuff."

"Is that right?" Sawyer asked, handing Jordan her finished latte.

"I guess the 'boring and useless' and 'exciting stuff' all depends on your personal tastes," Jordan glanced over at Georgia whose eyebrows were raised and they both shook with suppressed laughter. Sawyer watched them, amused. "But yeah, I guess it's right. Ryan, our boss, is more of a straight-line, anti-creative spirit who loves history and business writing; stuff he says makes a difference in the real world. Fortunately for us, he decided to hire two girls who are big fans of creativity. We're fantasy readers, so I got him talked into halving the business and travel sections, which we never sell *any* of, and we more than doubled the fantasy section. There are so many younger people in this town and they really seem starved for the stuff, so sales increased pretty significantly since we started ordering more of it, and he couldn't argue with the numbers." Jordan paused as she realized how much and how quickly she had been talking. It was totally unlike her to share this much but having Georgia next to her and the friendliness of Sawyer's chocolate brown eyes just seemed to draw it out of her. She took a drink from her latte and looked away embarrassedly. Georgia smiled at her knowingly and took the vanilla latte Sawyer offered her.

"I'm so glad to hear *all* of that," Sawyer said, leaning back against the counter. "I'm more of a creativity fan myself. Well, sci-fi more than fantasy. Space fascinates me. Back when I lived with my mom, I loved spending time out on the water in the evenings just staring up at the stars and imagining what might be up there. Mom said my time would have been better spent thinking about what was *actually* up there and not what *might* be up there. But that's just not as exciting, you know?"

"Absolutely," Jordan nodded. "Although, sometimes reality can be just as crazy as the stuff people imagine." She stopped short and took another hurried drink of her latte again. What was the matter with her, she thought exasperatedly? She had spent the last twelve years purposely avoiding speaking to people whenever possible for just this reason. In the last hour, she had talked this guy's ear off and alluded to her condition, not to mention started getting chummy with Georgia.

"That's true," Georgia nodded, and Jordan noticed she seemed to have a slightly commiserating look. She wondered if she was just sensing a friend's discomfort, or if what she said had affected her for some other reason. Regardless, she was happy when Georgia continued.

"It sounds like your mom and Ryan might get along great."

Jordan and Sawyer both laughed at that. "Georgia, you might be right about that," Sawyer agreed, still chuckling gently.

"So, Sawyer, you said you used to spend time out on the water when you lived with your mom. I assume that wasn't around here, since there's not much water to spend time on, except a lake or two. Are you new here? And if so, why did you decide to move here of all places?" Jordan asked. She decided to get him talking to take the attention away from herself and to give her less of an opportunity to ramble on and make a mess of things.

"Well, I was born and grew up on the southeast coast. It's a town called Waylea, South Carolina. We had a cabin right on the beach there because my dad was in the coast guard. Unfortunately, he passed away about ten years ago on the job, but by that point, our life was established there, and my mom didn't want me to change schools, so we stayed. After I graduated, mom started looking into moving back where she grew up, which is on the west coast. I debated going with her or staying in South Carolina, but then she got a letter from my grandfather; my dad's dad. She said he was really getting up there in years and couldn't work the land on his farm and his dairy operation quite as easily anymore, but she said he didn't seem to understand the word retirement. His letter asked if she knew if I was looking for work since he'd like to

31

keep the operation in the family if possible. He's a little bit reclusive and doesn't like to share his life with people who aren't family, not that I'd ever even met the man before. So, I weighed my options and, after looking into coast guard positions there in the Carolinas and being told there'd be no guarantee I'd be stationed there as they didn't currently have a need for anyone, I told her I'd love to help granddad if he'd have me. The rest is history. I got here a few years ago and settled into a routine on the farm. I never really came into town much; it was always granddad who came in for supplies or whatever we needed. He said he knew the vendors and had built up a working relationship with them. He didn't think they'd take a young guy seriously and I'd end up getting taken advantage of and losing us money." He shook his head at that, smiling. "But, after a *lot* of strong arming and years of work, I finally convinced him to get his operation a little more modernized and now it's running efficiently enough it doesn't take up as much of our time. However, it also doesn't pay great," he laughed. "So, I decided to come into town and get another little side job and, since I love coffee, I asked the grocer if he'd let me rent out a little space for a coffee stand." He held out his hands, gesturing around him. "And here I am."

"Wow," Georgia said. "Your mom must be really proud of what you've done here. Does she agree you made a good choice coming here?"

"She actually passed away as well, almost two years ago. Car accident. But before that happened, she was definitely glad things were heading in a good direction here. And, yeah, I think she thought I made the right decision."

Georgia nodded, looking embarrassed she had brought up painful memories and not sure what direction to steer the conversation at this point.

Jordan stepped in and helped her out. "Geez, that's a crazy hectic journey you've been on. Sorry about your parents by the way. That must've been hard. They'd definitely be proud of you though seeing all you've accomplished. Incidentally, who's your grandpa?" Jordan asked curiously. "Georgia just moved here, but I've lived here my whole life and know pretty much everyone in town."

"Uh… his name is Augustus Toole," Sawyer said, a bit sheepishly.

"Oh, wow," Jordan said, trying to hide her look and tone of distain. "Yeah, um, I know Mr. Toole. He's really… well, he uh… he sells great cheese."

Georgia burst into laughter at Jordan's comment. Sawyer smiled, clearing his throat a bit to hide a laugh himself. "Yeah, he's a bit of a character. I didn't figure I'd be too popular around here being the grandson of an old codger like Auggie Toole, but he's family," Sawyer shrugged. "What's a guy to do?"

"Oh, no one'll judge you for being his grandson," Jordan said quickly. "Heck, if we all judged each other for our family members' eccentricities in a town this small, no one would like anyone."

Sawyer did laugh at that. "Well, that's good to hear, because I wouldn't want you to judge me before you got to know me." His eyes didn't leave Jordan's face.

Georgia looked back and forth between them, grinning and drinking the last of her latte. "So, how much do I owe you," she finally said, pulling a coin purse out of her wallet.

Sawyer broke eye contact with Jordan and looked quickly at Georgia. "Oh, hey, don't worry about it. Consider it a welcome-to-the-neighborhood gift." He grinned and looked back to Jordan. "And you don't worry about it either. I have a feeling I'll need help navigating the socialization maze in this crazy town and I could use someone who knows the waters, so to speak. Consider it a bribe." He winked.

Jordan blushed lightly and felt the familiar cooling sensation in her chest. She smiled and took a deep breath, feigning deep thought and consideration of his proposal. When she finally felt the cooling sensation leave, she smiled and said "Ok, I guess I could help you out. Lord knows you have enough obstacles living with the Toole." All three of them laughed and the girls started making their way to the door.

"It was nice meeting you," Jordan said over her shoulder. "I'm sure we'll see each other quite a bit; especially the next few days."

"Definitely," Georgia said. "You're going to be responsible for keeping us sane. It's a *big* responsibility."

"I'm looking forward to it," Sawyer said, giving them a small wave, turning back to the stock room, and disappearing from sight.

"Well, that was interesting," Georgia said, keeping her face down so Jordan couldn't see her grinning.

"Yeah," Jordan said. "I can't remember the last time someone new came to town and now there are basically two of you in the same month. I know he's been here for years, but if we don't watch out, this town's population will be booming."

"No kidding. I'm just kind of glad I'm not the only newish person in town. It might keep some of the attention off me. I've never much enjoyed being the center of attention."

"Right," Jordan said. "Me either."

"I think you're out of luck there."

Jordan turned and looked confusedly at Georgia. "What do you mean?"

"I'm pretty sure you're going to be the center of Sawyer's attention." She smiled, wryly.

Jordan blushed again and shoved her shoulder into Georgia's. "Stop that," she laughed. "He was just being nice and hoping he could get some help making nice around town. Plus, you haven't met Mr. Toole. That guy's a nightmare. He's the grouchiest man I've ever met. He's about a hundred and fifty years old, can hardly hear, and has a heck of a temper. I feel bad for Sawyer. He's going to *need* a friend around here."

"Yeah, sure. A friend," Georgia said, shoving her shoulder back into Jordan's. "Whatever you need to tell yourself.

But hey, between meeting you and now Sawyer, it might not be too bad for me here. I'm actually really looking forward to being here now."

"That's good, because I'm looking forward to you being here, too." The girls smiled at each other as they reached their cars which were parked next to each other a little way down from the bookstore. "See you tomorrow!"

"Absolutely. See you then." They waved, got into their cars, and drove off in the same direction.

As Jordan drove the short distance home after Georgia turned off on her street, she thought about the events of the day. Between reminiscing back to the first day of her new secret life, to the cooling feeling shaking Georgia's hand, to being more open about her life with two complete strangers than she had ever been to the people she'd known her whole life, she felt like it was her first day of a new life all over again. She was going to have to be careful around these two. But, at the same time, it felt kind of nice being relaxed around them some of the time. Ok, so maybe not relaxed. Her thoughts went back to Sawyer's eyes and, once more, she felt that cooling sensation in her chest. She took a deep breath again and the cooling sensation changed to a warm one. She smiled and continued driving to her house.

Chapter Four
The Reset

"I love this place, I really do," Jordan said, breathing heavily and carrying a stack of fifteen thick books from the stock room. "But twenty-four hours over the last two days is taking its toll on me. I need to be somewhere that isn't here."

"I completely agree," Georgia said, putting the last book from her stack on the shelf and checking it off her list. "If someone comes in the next few days and wants a fantasy novel that *isn't* on one of these shelves, I may scream." She laughed and headed back to the stock room to grab the next pile.

"You won't be alone," Jordan called, sitting down cross-legged in front of the shelf she was stocking. "It all looked great on paper, but I feel I underestimated the amount of manual labor involved. It does feel good to be almost done, though."

"That's true, and it really looks great in here." Georgia's voice filtered out from the stockroom. "Sawyer's been a godsend keeping us in coffee these past two days. I think I'd have crashed at the end of yesterday without a caffeine fix. I mean, late-night coffee hasn't been amazing for my sleep schedule, but hey, plenty of time to sleep when you're dead, right?"

"Amen," Jordan said, standing up again and leaning back to stretch her back muscles. It had been almost a week since she'd been able to visit the woods and her lack of physical activity was causing her muscles to tense and cramp from non-use. "I'm looking forward to having tomorrow off. But, if things get crazy, don't be afraid to call me. I'll be home for a good chunk of the day tomorrow and I have no problem coming to bail you out if you need me."

"Thanks, but I'm sure I'll be fine. I feel pretty comfortable with the programs now, and Ryan will be here if I have questions. He could use some work now and then," she laughed, setting her stack of books on one of the rolling carts they were using to do heavy book transfers and pushing it back out to the shelves they were working on. "Plus, it's Sunday so it shouldn't be too busy and we aren't open late."

The bell above the door tinkled and both girls looked, not toward the door, but toward the clock above the stock room door. "It's 8:55pm. Who would be coming in five minutes before we close?" Jordan asked, somewhat irritably. She walked to the aisle to see who the offender was. Her face broke into a smile.

"I think I know who it is," Georgia laughed, turning and rolling the cart away from Jordan and toward the empty set of shelves a few rows over. "Tell him he's cutting it close tonight."

"I heard that," Sawyer said, coming into the aisle where Jordan was standing. "You think you might show a little more appreciation to your personal beverage delivery service," he said in mock injury.

"We definitely appreciate you!" Jordan said, taking the large coffee cup he held out to her. "We were just talking about how this schedule is really taking its toll on our cheery dispositions." She drank deep from the cup and sighed in pleasure. "This tastes amazing! What did you put in this time?"

"It's a cinnamon hazelnut mocha with a quad shot," he smiled. "I figured you could use the extra jolt *and* sugar for the home stretch tonight. I wouldve been over earlier, but there was a group of about eight girls that came in forty-five minutes ago and could *not* make up their minds what they wanted. They had to discuss the merits of non-fat milk in a mocha freeze latte versus two percent milk in a sugar free vanilla freeze latte. It was sickening," he huffed, handing the other large cup to Georgia who had just walked up to join them.

"Oh, yes. We're familiar with that crowd. They're the same crew that comes in every time the magazines update to catch up on the latest gossip about what's going on in the world; which celebrity is sleeping with/marrying/divorcing/knocking up the other. Ninety percent of them probably won't even make it out of this town. I don't know what difference it should make to them," Jordan said in disgust.

"My goodness, the bitter game *is* strong tonight, isn't it?" Sawyer joked and nudged her ribs gently with his elbow.

Jordan looked slightly remorseful and gazed down. "I'm sorry. That *was* a tad snarky. Being tired doesn't bring out my best side. But listen, we really do appreciate everything you've done the past couple of days. Multiple coffee deliveries in a day is above and beyond, for sure."

"Absolutely," Georgia agreed. "You really need to start letting us pay you though. You have to be bleeding money with this much coffee just walking out the door."

"Hey, it's no problem. Really. I'm actually using you guys as Guinea pigs to try out some new flavor combos. I took a leaf from your book, Jordan. I figured if you could get a guy like Ryan to come around and try something new, I could pitch the idea of having monthly drink specials with new flavors to try to pull in some extra business. I even did some research about ordering and waste inventories at other shops and found out what flavors sold best in what months and which ones didn't. I'm going to use the flavors that start slowing down as the features in those months to kind of level out sales and make it so there isn't as much wasted or expired inventory."

"Wow, that's a great idea!" Georgia exclaimed.

"Yeah, and way more thought went into your project than mine. I just looked at what was trending and added in some of my own biases when it came to ordering. You're going that creative extra mile. Ryan would hate you!" They all laughed.

"That's oddly high praise. Unfortunately, the creativity is coming more from necessity than anything else. The guy who originally set up my order quit suddenly, and the new kid doesn't seem to understand how to read the orders just yet, so I've been getting some very different stock than what I anticipated. After it happened twice, I went through order histories and that's where the project was born."

"That's frustrating," Georgia said. "Ryan had an issue the other day with his order not making it here at all. There must be a lot of turnover for some reason.

"I bet he reacted really well to that," Sawyer said and they all grinned. "Anyway, since you're doing me a favor and helping test out my stuff, I wouldn't feel right taking your money. Just think of the coffee as payment for being consultants." He smiled and headed to the door just as it opened and Ryan stepped in.

Sawyer nodded at him in acknowledgement and turned back to the girls. "See you tomorrow, Georgia. See you Monday, Jordan. Evenin', sir," he said to Ryan and waved as he walked out.

"Does that guy ever work? I feel like he spends as much time here as he does next door." Ryan said, closing the door and locking it.

"He keeps us in coffee and that keeps us civilized," Jordan said, narrowing her eyes at Ryan. "You should be thanking him. We'd be much less pleasant without his wares."

"You mean, what I've been dealing with is the warm and fuzzy pair of you? Lord, help us," he muttered and walked into the stock room. "It does, however, look like you've made good progress back here," he called. "Do you think you're going to have it finished up tonight?"

"Definitely," Georgia said. She and Jordan waited as he exited the stock room, then joined him as he went into his office. "We only have a couple piles of new stock left back there and then we just have to take the rolling carts full of the books we pulled from business and travel and put them in the stock room. We figured out a good method to store them until they're either wanted or it's time to send them back. *And* we made it so they won't take up much space. It involves stacking them spine side out and a lot of labels and unique organization, but we wrote it all down so we can be on the same page."

"Well, you know I'm not much for compliments, but you two have done a bang-up job with this reset. I still can't be excited about the material, but I'm looking forward to seeing the numbers this generates." He took off his blazer and laid it across the back of his computer chair. "Why don't I help you guys get the rest of the mind jelly books out to the floor so you both can work on setting up the re-stock however you see fit. Then maybe we can all get out of here at a decent time."

"Wow, you *are* in a good mood tonight, aren't you?" Jordan said, smiling amusedly. "Thanks, boss. It shouldn't take more than an hour and a half to two hours to have it all done and count the drawer."

"Let's do it!" Georgia said, punching her fist in the air and hustling off to the sales floor.

"She's had a lot of coffee," Jordan said by way of explanation. Ryan just shook his head and followed her out of his office.

They left the bookstore shortly after ten. The rest of the reset had gone smoothly, and Ryan had actually been helpful with shelving the new stock as well as pulling the books to go back in the stock room. It had started a little bit like watching a father choose which of his children to sacrifice, but when he got past the dramatics everything went quickly. They locked up the store and the girls waved goodbye to Ryan as he walked toward his house.

"I think I need to put in a request to Sawyer to switch me to decaf after noon. I'm still buzzed on caffeine. I won't be able to get to sleep until the sun comes up at this rate." Georgia said, bouncing slightly as they stood next to Jordan's car.

Jordan laughed. "I know what you mean. I'm definitely not feeling very tired right now either. I think it's a combo of the caffeine and the relief of being done with this reset. I can't wait to see what people think of it. I hope it has the effect I want. If it doesn't bring in at least fifteen percent more profit, Ryan will never let me hear it and I *really* don't want to have to put all those stupid books back on the shelf. That would be like a slap in the face."

"It's totally going to work," Georgia said, comfortingly. "You won't have to put any books back. In fact, I anticipate another reset in the next six to twelve months because we'll need even more room for the fantasy section. Heck, maybe we'll stop carrying other kinds of books all together!"

"You seriously need to chill," Jordan said. They both giggled. "And I really hope we don't have to do this again any time soon. This was exhausting!" They stood in the cool air a little longer, letting it relax them. "Hey, do you want a ride home? I just noticed your car isn't here."

"Yeah, my mom dropped me off today on her way to run some errands. I told her it wasn't too cold, so I'd just walk home whenever we got done, but a ride would actually be great. I may be wired now, but I have a feeling if the crash hits before I make it home I may have to just sleep in a dumpster." They both got in Jordan's car, snickering at the image of Georgia napping in a dumpster.

Ten minutes later, Jordan pulled into the driveway of Georgia's house. "I've driven by this place a thousand times, but never really looked at it. It's really pretty. How are you guys liking it here?"

"We love it! It's so roomy inside and the fireplace is my favorite. I think every home in New England should be required to have one. It makes the place smell great and mom's cold more often these days so she loves how cozy it feels."

"Yeah, cold is pretty standard here. How are you both doing? Getting settled in?" Jordan asked.

Georgia looked out the window at her house. It was a little while before she responded. "Well, she's more tired these days now that the treatments have stopped." Jordan looked at Georgia, her eyes wide and eyebrows raised. "She found out she was sick not too long before we moved here. She's still in good spirits, though." Georgia rushed on, and it was clear she didn't want to talk in depth about her mom's illness. "We laugh and have a great time. We play cards and board games and she still likes to cook supper every night and bake all kinds of delicious goodies, despite me offering to cook on my days off. She loves being a mom..." she trailed off.

"Loves being *your* mom." Jordan said, warmly. "I'm so sorry to hear she's sick. She's lucky to have such an amazing daughter. It's great you're getting to spend so much time with her." Just then, the front door swung open and a tall, very thin woman bundled in a huge coat walked out with a garbage bag in her hands.

Georgia threw her door open and jumped out of Jordan's car. "Mom, stop! I can take that out. I thought Mr. Onus was supposed to stop by and see if there was anything you needed before he headed to the mill."

"Oh, honey, it's fine," the lady replied with a dismissing wave of her hand. "He probably just got busy and couldn't make it. Besides, I can walk a little bag of garbage to the curb. You worry too much." Jordan got out of her car, leaving it running, and walked to the front of it just as Georgia's mom reached them. Georgia took the bag from her mother, who took a lock of her long hair and shook it, lovingly. She turned to Jordan. "This must be the lovely Jordan I've heard so much about. I'm Amy." She reached her hand out and Jordan took it gently. She could feel every bone in Amy's hand and it was absolutely freezing, but she gripped Jordan's hand firmly and shook it before letting go.

"It's nice to meet you too, Ms. Linden." Jordan smiled.

"Please, call me Amy. Would you like to come in and have some sugar cookies? They just came out of the oven."

"Oh, that's nice of you, but I should probably get home. It's getting late…"

"Nonsense," Amy laughed. "It's only a little after ten on a weekend. It's the perfect time for warm sugar cookies and milk in front of the fire. Plus, I'd love to chat and get to know you a little. I've hardly had a chance at all to reacquaint myself with the town and talk to people. Georgia speaks so highly of you. Please, just for a little while?"

Jordan met Georgia's gaze. "She does make the best sugar cookies around," Georgia said with a grin.

"Then, I guess I'd be a fool to turn them down." She walked back to the open driver's side door, reached in to turn off the ignition, and put her keys in her pocket. "Cookies and conversation it is!"

"Oh, I'm so glad!" Amy said, putting her arm around Jordan's waist. There was almost nothing to her, but she had surprising strength as she guided Jordan up the path to the front door. "This will be a fun girl's night." Jordan looked to her right and saw the smile on Georgia's face as she looked back at her. She clearly loved seeing her mother this happy.

"Sounds great," Jordan said, and they walked inside.

Chapter Five
Secret Revealed

Jordan was lying balanced on a moss-covered log near the bank of the pond in the clearing. It had been weeks since she'd been able to make her way into the woods and it felt great to be back. She had made the decision to stay close to town and to a phone until she knew Georgia had gotten the hang of everything at the book store. She hadn't wanted to miss a call in case she had any issues. She needn't have worried, though. Georgia was a natural at picking up the flow of things and no calls had come. Jordan finally accepted she wouldn't likely be needed and whatever questions might arise, Ryan could handle, so she had taken off after eating an early lunch and had been lounging by the lake for hours. The few late afternoon sunbeams that were able to penetrate the thick canopy overhead took the edge off the chill in the air as they hit the skin on her arms and face. Fall was definitely in the air and soon the leaves would be falling. She had heard people from all over the country traveled to the New England area to see the seasons change, but apparently none of them thought enough of their little town to ever visit it. Not that she was upset by this. In her opinion, the less people around, the better. She sat up, putting one foot on the ground and hugging her other knee to her chest. It was true, though, that the quality of people in town had sure improved in the past few weeks, she thought. For the first time she could remember, she had a real friend; one she felt she could tell almost anything too. Amy had proved to be a wonderful woman and she could see where Georgia got her kindness and humor. The three of them had spent quite a few nights over the last few weeks talking, eating amazing pastries, and playing cards or board games. First, they had just discussed the normal introductory topics, but they had quickly slipped into conversation about anything and everything (well, almost everything) like they had all known each other for years. Jordan was even considering asking Georgia over for supper one night soon. She had mentioned Georgia enough that her mother and father had been asking if they were ever going to get to meet her, and she really didn't have a real reason why they shouldn't, especially with all the time she was spending with Amy.

And then there was Sawyer. Jordan smiled as the cooling feeling started in her chest and her heart rate elevated ever so slightly. He was easy to talk to as well. Almost *too* easy, she thought. He had a way of speaking and looking at her that made her just want to say anything and everything that was on her mind, and that was dangerous. Yet, still, she found herself drawn to him. She looked out at the blue water of the pond as it reflected the green canopy above them and the dark brown of the trees. She pictured his soft, brown eyes gazing into hers. Even Georgia had continued to pick up on their apparent connection the few times the three of them had spent time together, though it wasn't a topic she and Jordan ever discussed at any length. When Georgia mentioned him and that he seemed to like her, Jordan would steer the topic in another direction as quickly as possible. Fortunately, Georgia never pushed. It was another way in which she was a great friend; she knew how to read a situation and when to let something go.

A loud snap and a rustling brought Jordan to her feet. She stood and looked around, letting her heightened senses explore her surroundings far beyond just her line of sight.

The smell was familiar, and she searched her mind for what it was. Not a deer, she thought. She listened hard and heard the faintest of footfalls; two sets of them. One was light and very quick; a person. The other was also quick but differently gaited. A quadruped for sure, and a heavy one. She breathed in more deeply. A bear, she thought. This wasn't good.

She assessed the sound and took off in a direction that would lead her to intercept the person and bear's current path. Perhaps if she could catch the bear's attention enough to frighten it off, she would be able to stop what had the potential to be a devastating situation. Jordan arrived at the top of a large hill that crested a steep ravine in the woods and stopped. She could hear the person's ragged breathing before she saw them. Whoever it was sounded as though they had been running for a while. Just then, she saw a girl emerge through the trees approximately a hundred yards away from her on the opposite crest, catch her foot on a root, and go crashing down the hillside into the ravine. Jordan's heart sank as she recognized the girl. It was Georgia! What in the world was she doing this far into the woods?! Jordan had told her she liked coming into the woods to relax and get her mind off things, but she had also warned her the woods housed quite a few dangerous animals and it was very easy to get lost in them. She had promised to take her in them sometime and show her around, but she never thought Georgia would ever wander this far on her own.

Jordan cursed under her breath. She watched as Georgia came to a stop, pulled herself to her feet, and whipped around to look behind where she had just fallen. Before Jordan could call to her and beckon her to run toward her, the bear emerged through the trees. It paused at the top of the ridge, then began to navigate its way down toward Georgia. Jordan was breathing hard, both with anger for the situation Georgia had gotten herself into, and out of fear for her friend's safety. She knew there was no way she could take on a bear as herself, especially when it was on the rampage as this one was. Georgia had clearly scraped herself up during her run through the woods and her fall down the embankment, because Jordan could smell the metallic scent of blood. And if she could smell it, the bear definitely could too. Just as she had all but made up her mind to transform and do what she could to help her friend, Georgia turned to find an escape route and her eyes locked on Jordan. Their eyes met, and shock flooded Georgia's eyes.

"Jordan?!" she exclaimed, her tone one of mixed fear and surprise.

Jordan didn't say anything. She couldn't change now. No one could know what she was and what she could do. There were too many things that could go horribly wrong if anyone found out. Just because Georgia hadn't told anyone about her suspicions that Jordan liked Sawyer more than she was letting on, didn't mean she would keep something as huge as her new friend being able to change into a wolf to herself. Jordan's eyes darted around the woods, wracking her brain for any other option that would result in Georgia not becoming bear food. Nothing immediate came to her.

"Jordan!" Georgia screamed again, this time nothing but fear and panic registered in her voice. She was stumbling her way up the hill in Jordan's direction, her gaze darting back and forth between the bear and Jordan. In a split second, Jordan made her decision. She would try to get Georgia to safety first before she risked revealing her secret. She half ran, half fell down the hill until she reached Georgia. She grabbed her friend's hand and pulled her along behind her back up the hill.

"Come on," she urged. "That bear has to go down the hill slowly, but it's going to go up this side quicker than we can. We need to try to get out of its line of sight and hide somewhere quietly. We might be able to ditch him that way."

"Why does it have to go down the hill slowly?" Georgia gasped, stumbling after Jordan.

"Bears' hind legs are longer than their front legs, so going down a hill is difficult and awkward for them. But that awkwardness disappears when it comes to running uphill. You got lucky stumbling down that ravine. We might have enough of an edge to get away." Jordan's legs, although conditioned, were already starting to burn with the combined effort of climbing the hill and pulling Georgia behind her. She hoped they both had enough strength left in them to find somewhere to hide. As they reached the top of the hill, she chanced a look behind her and her heart contracted in fear. The bear was almost to the bottom of the hill. They were only going to have about a twenty-second head start. She let go of Georgia's hand and yelled for her to follow her and not look back. She ran through thick patches of ground cover and dense trees, trying to get out of view of the bear when it reached the top. After a few thick patches, she found a clear path and tore off toward her pond. If they could get there in time, they could possibly camouflage themselves in the willow branches.

It was then that she heard the crash just a few feet behind them and heard the grunting breaths of the bear behind them. The little hope she had started to fade. As they broke into the clearing of her pond, Jordan braced herself and made up her mind. She stopped short and pushed Georgia on as she caught up to her.

"Keep going!" she screamed. "Don't stop until you're behind the willow branches. I'll meet you there." Georgia slowed down for the briefest of seconds, but Jordan shoved her harder. "I'm serious, go!" Georgia turned and ran toward one of the curtains of willow branches on the opposite side of the pond.

As the bear entered the clearing, Jordan took a deep breath and concentrated, allowing herself to feel the cooling sensation that had already been fighting to take over and let it spread through her body. She felt the transformation begin, and let her body twist and bend to adapt to its new shape. She opened her eyes as her front feet hit the ground and saw the bear had paused at the sight of her transformation. She had been banking on that paused and she growled deeply and bared her teeth, advancing on the bear slowly. The bear let a guttural rumble escape its throat and pulled itself up onto its back legs in an attempt to make itself look bigger and more formidable. It might have worked with a regular forest creature, but Jordan was on a mission to save her friend and it wasn't going to work with her. She let out a snarling bark and ran toward the bear. It quickly dropped down to all fours again. It paused just a moment as if making up its mind to fight or not, and in that moment of indecision, Jordan leaped and hit it square in the shoulder. She didn't weigh much less as a wolf than she did as a human and her momentum was enough to knock it on its side. She whipped her head around and bit down hard just behind the bear's ear. The bear let out a roar of pain and anger, rolling her off. She was already prepared though and maintained her footing. She spun around and got low on her front legs in preparation for another rush. The bear got back to its feet as well, but apparently the disappearance of one meal and the transformation of another into an animal that was prepared to put up a hell of a fight wasn't a good enough reason to continue the battle. The bear backed up a few steps. Jordan stood back up out of her crouch and growled again. The bear huffed a breath and turned away, lumbering off back through the trees which they had just come.

Jordan kept her eye on the tree line the bear had disappeared through and listened hard to make sure it didn't decide to change its mind. When she could no longer hear footsteps steps and the smell had faded from the air, she turned and looked toward the willow curtain. She had options. She could just leave and hope Georgia hadn't seen her. But what would she say to her if, when she next saw her, she asked her about it? Or worse, what if she told everyone about it before Jordan even got back into town? Maybe she could convince her she had clearly fainted and dreamt what she saw happen to Jordan in her unconsciousness. Or that she had been so stressed and scared she had begun hallucinating things. Jordan looked down at the ground and took a deep breath. She started taking steps toward the willows when she noticed something odd. She could no longer smell Georgia. Had she taken off further than the willows to hide? She wouldn't blame her if she had. Getting as far away as possible from a rampaging bear made complete sense to her.

Just then, another smell reached her nose. She had smelled this before, but she couldn't place it. It wasn't a common smell in her woods. She began looking around and listening hard to locate the source. She could tell it was close by the strength of the smell, and yet there was nothing in her clearing.

"Up here," she heard a familiar voice say, softly. Jordan raised her head to scope out the trees. At first, she saw nothing, but then she made out a large, dark figure about 20 feet up hidden well in the leaves of a large tree. She walked closer to the tree and saw it was a large bobcat. Jordan tilted her furry head in complete confusion. In the twelve years she had been transforming in these woods, she had never been able to communicate with another animal; not even the few other wolves she had come across. And why would this bobcat sound almost exactly like Georgia? Maybe she was the one hallucinating, Jordan thought to herself.

"Georgia?" Jordan said, tentatively. She could hear the sound she made was like a soft, high-pitched whine, but she also heard the questioning name she had asked the bobcat.

There was no response, but the bobcat shifted in the tree and began making its way down the branches. Jordan watched as the creature got closer to the ground. About six feet away, it jumped and landed lightly a few feet away from her. They stared at each other for a minute before the bobcat's mouth opened slightly and Jordan heard her speak again.

"This can't be real," the big cat said softly, in what was unmistakably Georgia's voice. "It just can't be true that someone else can do this; that *you* can do this."

Jordan ungracefully sank onto her back haunches. She couldn't believe it either. How could it be that someone else had same ability she had kept secret most of her life? After twelve years, she still had a hard time believing her *own* abilities were real and not just a recurring dream or hallucination. She had kept this secret to herself for so long, believing she was the only one who could possibly be like this. She had held off getting close to anyone for fear of leaking a clue about her condition because she *knew* this wasn't happening to anyone else and no one could possibly understand. And now, here she was, sitting in front of another someone just like her! It was almost too much to take in.

"Jordan?" Georgia asked again. "Are you ok? Are you hurt?" She took a tentative step toward Jordan and then sat on her haunches as well.

"I… I think I'm ok," Jordan said after another thirty seconds or so. "I just… I can't believe this is happening."

"Me either," Georgia said. "Why don't we get back to ourselves and go somewhere private for a chat. I mean, somewhere private that doesn't have angry bears and God know what else to watch out for."

"Sure," Jordan said. "I guess that'd be ok. I think I need a minute to be able to clear my head enough to do it though. Give me a few."

"Sure, absolutely." Georgia rose and walked to the pond. Jordan watched her as she bowed her head down and then slowly transitioned back into a girl, sitting on the bank of the pond, looking out over the water.

Jordan got up and walked the perimeter of the clearing for a couple minutes until her heart rate regulated and she felt a bit calmer. She finally took a deep breath and willed her transition back to her human form. She shook out her arms and legs which were still a little sore from running up the hill and from the brief encounter with the bear. She squatted and stood up again a few times to stretch out her leg muscles and then locked her fingers and raised her arms over her head, stretching her arm and shoulder muscles as well.

"Are you really ok?" Georgia asked over her shoulder. "Sorry," she said sheepishly as she saw Jordan jump at the sound off her voice. "I didn't mean to startle you."

"It's fine," Jordan said with a wave of her hand. "I'm a bit on edge after… well, after everything."

"I totally understand. Listen, I know this is crazy and weird and awkward as hell. But a part of me is so incredibly relieved to know I'm not alone in this. I didn't think anyone could ever know what this is like. I mean, I was prepared to let that bear get me rather than letting you know this about me. I figured there was no way you'd want to be friends with a freak and you'd tell everyone. I couldn't bear telling mom we had to leave where she wanted to come back to so badly. I've feared that my whole life. It's why…"

"You never made friends." Jordan finished. Georgia smiled and nodded gently. "Same here. I figured staying distant would keep me and everyone else more comfortable and I'd be safer. I didn't want anyone experimenting on me and having to live the rest of my life in a science lab or something."

"Exactly," Georgia nodded. "So, what do you think? Do you want to grab something to eat or drink and then maybe talk more about this? I think it's probably better we get this discussion out of the way, right?"

"I do, but I don't really want to go to town right now," Jordan said. "How would you feel about coming back to my place and talking? I can make us some coffee and my mom made a great fruit salad yesterday. I could make us some sandwiches too, and then we can chat as long as we need."

"That sounds great," Georgia said. Then with apprehension in her voice she asked "So, you still want to be friends?"

Jordan paused and then turned to Georgia, grinning a bit, and per her arm around her friend's shoulders. "Well, with us possibly being the only two of this particular brand of freak in existence, I think we should probably stick together, don't you?"

Georgia laughed and put her arm around her friend's waist. "I couldn't agree more!"

They walked slowly together out of the clearing and toward the trail that would take them back to Jordan's house.

Chapter Six
History

"I don't even know where to begin," Georgia said, her hands wrapped around a warm mug of coffee. Two empty bowls that had once contained heaping piles of fruit salad sat empty; one in front of each of the girls. Crumbs from their sandwiches were all that was left on their plates. The coffee, however, was still brewing. They were on their second pot. Through it all, neither of them had breached the subject of the strange events of the day. "I know we need to talk about it. I've just had literally no practice on how to even start this conversation."

Jordan nodded, taking another drink of her coffee. The warmth from the liquid helped cover the lingering cool feeling in her chest. She knew what Georgia meant. She had never told a soul what she could do. She had never even uttered the words out loud before. It almost seemed like it was forbidden, even though they each knew the other had the exact same secret and the exact same concerns. It was obvious neither would tell anyone, and yet something was stopping them from discussing it. But someone had to breach the topic. She looked up at her friend and began.

"I've spent twelve years convincing myself telling someone about this would cause nothing but problems. I've never told anyone about it. I've hid it from everyone. And the fact that you're in the same boat makes me think anything I *do* say will just be stating the obvious. So, I don't really know where to begin either."

"Wait," Georgia said, setting down her mug, her eyebrows knitted together. "What do you mean twelve years? You've only been able to change for the past twelve years?"

"Yeah," Jordan responded, a bit surprised by Georgia's confusion. After all, weren't they dealing with the same situation? "I was ten years old and I was in the woods. It was hot, and I was soaking my feet in the pond. Then when I got up, a bear showed up, a lot like today, and I was so scared that I started shaking and my heart started racing. All of a sudden, it was like I was vibrating or something and the next thing I knew, everything got taller and I had four furry legs and a tail. The bear took off and I looked in the pond and saw my reflection was a wolf. That was the first time it happened." Jordan found that once she started talking about it, it became easier. "After that, I thought I was going to have to either go back to town and try to figure out how to fix it, or just live in the woods forever as a wolf. But once I calmed down, I was able to change back. I spent months coming back to the woods almost every day, learning how to transform at will as well as how to try to prevent it when I got scared or upset or angry. I have it pretty much under control by now, but I try to avoid tense situations just in case. But I still don't know what caused it to happen."

Georgia just looked at Jordan for a while and then shook her head and picked up her mug again. "That's insane! I don't know *what* I would've done in that situation. I don't know that I ever would've been able to calm down enough to work through it or change back. And your parents didn't know or help you or anything?!"

"No. I couldn't bring myself to tell them. I wanted to a lot when I was younger, but in the back of my mind I always worried they'd either feel like they needed to take me to a doctor, or worse, a psychiatrist. It's hard for *me* to believe this is all really happening, and I'm the one *living* it. I wouldn't blame them for not being able to believe it. And I definitely couldn't show them. It would give them a heart attack." Jordan shook her head. "It was better no one knew anything."

"Oh, I totally understand your reasoning. It's just, I've been able to change ever since I can remember, but my mom helped me understand it and learn how to control it."

"You mean Amy can change, too?! Or your dad? Is it genetic? It is some kind of illness or some kind of mutation situation?"

Georgia held up a hand to slow Jordan's line of questions. "No, she couldn't do it herself, but she said she'd been close to someone when she was younger who was able to do it and they told her all about it. She never mentioned dad being able to do it, so I don't think it was him. I guess I was just lucky she knew about it and could guide me through it all. But she told me the same things you figured out on your own; that I couldn't tell anyone or they might want to have me tested and experiment on me or that others might just think I was crazy. Even worse, someone could fear I was dangerous and shoot me or something. So we just kept to ourselves. She would teach me in the small wooded area behind our house late at night. No one ever came in there because it was private land, so we were pretty safe."

"So, Amy never told you what caused it or what it all meant that this was happening to you? She never gave any clue about the origin of it all?"

"I'm sorry, Jordan, but no, she never told me anything like that. I asked her of course, when I was really young. She just said it was an extremely rare gift and I was special to be able to do it, but I needed to guard my abilities from those who wouldn't understand. She always focused more on how to deal with a situation, any situation, and not as much on how the situation had come about."

Jordan was disappointed she wasn't any closer to figuring out what caused her ability to change, but she liked hearing about Georgia's situation. "Are you going to tell her about me now that you know?

"I don't know. I guess I hadn't really thought about it. I won't if you don't want me to."

"I don't mind if you do. I figure if she's kept your secret your whole life she can probably be trusted with mine. I wish I'd had a parental figure to help me through it all. I honestly feel relieved to have someone know about it; like I'm less of a freak or something. I was such a mess in the beginning. I'd be stuck as a wolf for hours sometimes. Other times, I wasn't able to change at all. It was really frustrating. I mean, it worked out ok, I guess. It just would've been easier with someone to help; some support.

Georgia leaned back and shook her head, smiling. "I still can't believe you did it all on your own. You're incredible."

Jordan smiled shyly. "I sure didn't feel incredible for a long time. I still don't, really. I mean, I have a really weird ability that I can't tell anyone about and that doesn't really do anything to help anyone. In fact, it keeps me isolated from everyone. It kind of seems more like a curse."

"It sure wasn't a curse today! I would've died if you hadn't been out there at just the right time. And your 'weird' ability definitely did something to help *me* today! What made you decide to reveal yourself anyway?"

"I don't know," Jordan looked down, suddenly self-conscious. "You're the first real friend I've ever had. Ever since I shook your hand the first day we met, I felt like we had a bond. Whenever I am about to change I get a feeling in my chest. It's kind of like a…"

"Cold feeling?" Georgia interjected, and Jordan nodded.

"Yeah. It almost always starts in my chest or stomach. But when I shook your hand that first day, I got the cool feeling in my hand when it touched yours. I didn't think much about it then, but it makes a lot of sense now. It's almost like I could sense a kindred spirit before I even knew how alike we were."

"I totally felt it, too!" Georgia exclaimed. "I've never felt it with anyone else either, although I've never met another person who had our gift."

"Curse," Jordan countered, a wry smile on her face.

"Po-ta-to, po-tah-to," Georgia said, laughing lightly. "But I never made the connection with the cold feeling during our hand shake and the transformation. I guess maybe I just thought you had cold hands or something." She shrugged. "I'm not always the most observant person. We can call it a character flaw."

"Hey, I'm not judging. I didn't put it together either until a bobcat in the woods knew my name and spoke with the voice of my best friend."

"I was so scared to do that," Georgia said, her eyes wide. "I didn't know if you were going to react well. I didn't even know if it would work. Any time I've tried to talk to other animals, it didn't work. Even other bobcats couldn't understand me."

"Same here," Jordan said. "Which is why I thought I was losing my mind for a minute. And then it almost seemed too good to be true that someone else could do this and that that someone was my friend. It still seems too good to be true."

"It does," Georgia nodded. "But you know what? We've lived too long distancing ourselves from others. I never made friends, never went to parties, I missed my prom, and I've never had a boyfriend. I feel like I missed out on a lot of normal childhood and teenage things because of this. I think it's time we both let ourselves have a life! Now that we have someone to talk to about literally *everything*, maybe we can be a little more..."

"Normal?" Jordan asked. They looked at each other and burst into laughter. The heaviness of the day melted away with the sound, and they both began to relax. After a bit, they regained their composure and sat in a comfortable silence.

"So," Georgia said, getting up and refilling her coffee mug. "Now that you've decided to be normal, are you going to celebrate by finally going on a date with coffee boy?" Jordan threw a balled-up napkin at Georgia, who caught it and grinned at her. "I mean, come on. It isn't like he's going to guess your secret. He's a really nice guy, he's obviously into family what with helping his grouchy old grandpa, he's essentially working two jobs so you know he's not lazy, he makes a mean cup of coffee, he's cute…" She paused. "And it's so obvious you like each other. He can't stop looking at you every time you're together."

"You know," Jordan said, taking the last drink out of her mug and holding it out for Georgia to refill. "Just because we *can* talk about anything, doesn't mean we're *going* to." Georgia gave her a knowing smile and winked, taking the mug and pouring a fresh cup. Jordan rolled her eyes and smiled back. "I don't know," she said, contemplatively. "Maybe I'll think about it."

"You do that," Georgia said, handing her mug back to her. "Because from what I've seen around here, I don't think you're going to do much better. It's clear to me the outsiders bring a lot to this town," she said haughtily, and they both laughed again.

"When you're right, you're right," Jordan said. "What was it like where you're from anyway?"

"Oh, it wasn't too different from here honestly. It was a small town. Everyone knew everyone and everyone's business. My mom's family was originally from here, as you know. But when my dad died in a mill accident just before I turned two, she was overcome with grief. He was the only family she had left, other than me of course. When I got older and asked about it, she told me she couldn't bear to stay where they'd shared a life; that it was too painful for her. So, she packed up our stuff and we moved. I don't know how she picked or found the town we moved to, but it was nice enough. We were always kind of outsiders there, but they treated us fine. They didn't make a lot of effort to get to know much about us, which was ok with us considering the huge secret we were trying to keep under wraps. So I grew up, went to school there, got decent grades, and participated in enough things to be able to fit in comfortably."

Here Georgia's voice softened and she paused for a bit before continuing. "It was right when I graduated that mom found out she was sick. She went to doctors in town and even in some of the bigger cities that were close to us, but the treatments they tried didn't work. When they told her there was nothing more they could do, mom said we'd be moving back to her hometown. She hasn't really told me why it was important to her for us to come back here, but I could tell she felt strongly about it, so I just went along with it. I just want her to be happy with the time she has left." Georgia trailed off, looking at her hands wrapped around her mug.

"I'm so sorry, Georgia. That must've been terrible for her, and for you. I know this place isn't so bad, but I can't imagine someone coming back if they were lucky enough to get out once. It hasn't happened since I can remember. And I can only think of two people that have left in a really long time. But, I suppose it also makes sense to come back somewhere familiar to spend the rest of your life."

"She always worked doing housecleaning when she and dad were dating and up until we moved. When dad died, he left her enough we could live comfortably if we lived modestly, so she didn't need to worry about finding work when we moved, although she still cleaned houses here and there, especially around the holidays. She's one of those crazy types that likes to clean. I think it's therapeutic for her or something; it relaxes her. Anyway, I think living here is about the cheapest of anywhere she could think of. And even though she doesn't have family left here and there are some sad thoughts of dad, this probably still feels like home. Plus, I'm glad she did," Georgia said, sitting in her chair. "Otherwise we wouldn't have met."

"That's true," Jordan smiled. "I'm sure it won't be that bad either. Even though this is a small town like the one you moved from, and everyone does know everyone else, we're all pretty good at keeping out of each other's business. I'll keep anyone from bugging you too much if they get the idea to do so. My mom'll probably look out for Amy, too. It won't take long until you guys get settled in and everyone'll get used to you. Plus, Sawyer's newish, or at least new to town, so everyone who bothers to pay any attention will be divided." Jordan reached across the table and squeezed Georgia's hand. "It'll be fine." She smiled, and Georgia smiled back.

"Thanks, Jordan. I appreciate that." She set her empty mug down. "So, your family's been here forever I take it?"

"I think so," Jordan answered, getting up from the table and going to the coffee pot. "I mean, I've never lived anywhere else and my parents have never talked about any of our family living anywhere else. I know my grandparents are dead and my parents both met here. Do you want one more cup? We can each have one more to finish the pot."

"Sure," Georgia said, looking at the clock. "I should probably get home in a half hour or so, but I have time for one more cup."

Jordan poured the coffee and brought the mugs back to the table. "My mom has worked at the school library since I was born. My dad was a police officer but he's pretty much retired now. He only works one or two days a week. He spends a lot of time in his shed doing woodworking now. Generally, the men around here end up working at the mill if they aren't in a public service job or manual labor position. It's weird because the mill doesn't seem big enough or to put out enough stuff to warrant needing that many people, but they're always hiring people. The women tend to take up the rest of the positions in shops around town, and every now and then, one of them will go to work at the mill as well. I don't know why, and it doesn't make much sense, but I kind of feel proud that neither of my parents fit the status quo of this town," she laughed. "Not that there's anything wrong with those things, but I like being different."

"Clearly," they both said at the same time. They were still laughing at this when the front door opened and closed, and two set of footsteps made their way to the kitchen doorway.

"I thought I heard voices in here," a pretty, brunette woman said, pulling off her coat and hanging it on a hook by the cabinet. "See, Hun, they were real voices, not the ones you say are in my head" she said over her shoulder as a tall, muscled man entered the room behind her.

"Ah, well you were bound to get lucky one of these days I suppose," he said, his eyes crinkling at the sides as he smiled.

"Hi, Mom, Dad. This is Georgia. Georgia, this is my mom, Judy, and my dad, Gordon."

"It's so nice to finally meet you," Judy said, squeezing Georgia's shoulders as she walked behind her toward the fridge. "Jordan has told us so much about you."

"Yes, hello Georgia," Gordan said, extending his large hand which engulfed hers as he shook it.

"It's nice to meet you both," Georgia said. "I'm sorry to stop by unannounced, but Jordan and I ran into each other in the neighborhood and decided to have some coffee and chat before I headed home."

"Oh, don't be silly!" Judy exclaimed, uncapping the bottle of water she had just retrieved and taking a drink. "You're welcome here anytime; announced or not."

"Absolutely," agreed Gordon, taking the offered bottle from Judy and drinking himself. "I'm afraid I need to be getting to bed soon. I have an early morning tomorrow, but I hope we can visit longer the next time you come around."

"That sounds great!" Georgia smiled.

"I thought you had tomorrow off," Jordan said as Gordon placed a kiss on top of her head. "Why do you need to get up early?"

"I did have the day off, but Sanders hasn't shown up for his shift the past two days and they don't think he will tomorrow either. They can't afford to have light coverage on that end of town for so many days; it's running the other guys ragged trying to make up ground. I offered to help them out until they can figure out who to shift around."

"Your dad's a wonderful man, but he doesn't quite understand the concept of retirement," Judy teased.

"Partial retirement," Gordon corrected her. "And I do understand the concept. But I also understand being there for your squad when they need help."

Judy nodded. "I know, Gordon, I'm just giving you a hard time. We're going through a similar situation at work. Two people quit unexpectedly this week, so we're delegating as well. I'm going in tomorrow morning to help sort the schedule. Have a good night girls."

"It does sound like you two have some busy days ahead of you," Georgia sympathized. She stood and slid her chair in. "Thanks for your hospitality Mr. and Mrs. Maren. I need to be going myself."

"Please, call us Gordon and Judy," Jordan's dad said. "I hope you're not rushing off on our account. You really can stay as long as you'd like."

"That's really nice of you, Gordon, but my mom'll be wondering where I am. I'll definitely come back and visit again soon."

"We look forward to it," Judy said, giving a small wave. "Jordan, honey, please lock up before you go to bed."

"I will. G'night Mom, Dad." They both waved and headed back to their bedroom.

Jordan and Georgia walked to the front door, stopping in the entryway.

"They seem really nice," Georgia said, warmly. "You're lucky to have them both in your life." Jordan didn't know how to respond to that since Georgia only had her mom, who was clearly very ill at this point. She just gave her a small smile and nodded. They were both quiet for a minute before Georgia rushed on. "I know you don't want to talk about it," she said. "But in the sake of normalcy, I really do think you owe it to yourself to try to see where things go with Sawyer. He seems to live outside the box, which you've just said you appreciate. I think he has a lot to offer. And he *is* crazy about you. It's pretty obvious. I'm not wrong, am I? You like him too, don't you?" Jordan looked at her but didn't say anything. "Come on. We can tell each other anything, remember? I'm never going to say a word to anyone."

Jordan sighed and leaned against the wall. "I guess he's a pretty great guy. He was so helpful during the reset. And he's easy to talk to. I just don't know. What's the point of getting close to someone like that? I can never tell him about my secret... *our* secret, I guess." She grinned. "That still feels good to say; 'our' secret. Feeling alone was getting a little old..."

"It was," Georgia agreed. "But, if you can't open yourself up to others, you're going to be alone forever. I'm only good to you for so much," she winked, and Jordan let out a bark of laughter. "But seriously, you've done an amazing job of hiding it this far, and now you have me to talk to about this kind of thing. So," she lowered her voice, "maybe you can talk to him about literally *everything* else and save the freaky dog/cat transformation stuff for me?"

Jordan kept her smile and nodded. "You're probably right. Ok," she said, standing upright again and squaring her shoulders. "Maybe I *will* see where things go with him. I mean, if things don't work out, I won't need to worry about telling him anything. If they do... we can cross that bridge when we come to it."

"I think that's a great plan." Georgia said. She paused a second and then leaned in to hug her friend. The cooling feeling spread everywhere they touched but neither girl pulled away. It was the first time either of them had hugged someone that wasn't a parent and the connection was a wonderful feeling. When they finally let go, the cooling feeling slowly died away.

"I should get going." Georgia zipped her jacket and reached for the doorknob.

"Hey," Jordan said, suddenly remembering something. "Where's your car? Weren't you coming from the far side of the woods when we ran into each other today? Do you want a ride back to it?"

"Oh, no thanks. My mom drove me to work this morning and then I just left from the bookstore when I got off and came straight into the woods from town. I was going to see if I could find the clearing you told me about, but I must have got turned around. I was thinking of the woods behind our house back home and took a wrong turn. My car's still at home and I'm not too far from here. I think the walk in the cool air will help me calm down and I may actually be able to sleep some tonight."

They stared at each other for a beat. "Probably not" they said, simultaneously.

Jordan watched as her friend walked away into the darkness. She closed the door, locked it, and turned around to lean against it. She looked at the clock on the wall. Hopefully a nice shower and some music would help her relax enough to be able to get some sleep this evening. She took a deep breath and walked toward her room. Taking into consideration the crazy events that had started her evening, it had been a pretty great night in the end and she was looking forward to seeing how things played out for her and Georgia. Her thoughts drifted to their brief discussion of Sawyer and she felt her cheeks redden slightly as she smiled. Her friend had been right; she really did enjoy spending time with him. Maybe she *could* do normal if she put her mind to it.

Chapter Seven
Normal

"Jordan!" Ryan called from his office.

Jordan shook her head and smiled apologetically at the woman she was ringing up at the counter. "I'm so sorry Mrs. Krantz; he doesn't always think to use the phone. He prefers that one-on-one contact. Anyway, I have a feeling your granddaughter will love this series. If she doesn't though, please feel free to bring it back and we can try another one. And, if I'm right and she *is* a fan, there are four more books in this series and I know a few other series with similar themes. It should keep her busy for a while! Thank you for your business and I hope to see you again soon!"

As Mrs. Krantz left the store, the bell above the door sounding her exit, Jordan set her jaw and walked back to Ryan's office.

"So, hey, here's an idea," she said, not bothering to knock or signal her arrival in any way. Her annoyance was only slightly improved by seeing him jump at the sound of her voice. "Perhaps if you're going to bellow across the store like a wounded buffalo, you might want to check to see if the store's empty first. Old lady Krantz was in looking for a book series for her granddaughter; the oldest one. If I can get on her good side, she has three more grandkids after that she could come in to buy things for. I didn't bring in all this extra business for you to drive them all out again with your lack of social etiquette. Now, what was so important it didn't warrant a phone call?"

Ryan rolled his eyes at her but didn't comment on his choice of communication. "I asked you to bring me the shipping list and the order for this week. I've looked all over my desk and I can't find them."

Jordan picked up two folders from a tray on his desk labeled "In" and held them out to him. "Forgive me. I figured you wanted things coming *in* to you in the 'in' folder on your desk. In the future, I'll just throw them in here haphazardly so you can find them more easily. Anything else?"

"What's your damage today, Jordan?" Ryan said, taking the folders from her and looking almost genuinely concerned. "You've been short and snarky all day. More so than usual, I mean."

Jordan took a breath and willed her shoulders to relax. Despite the shower, music, and pleasant enough dreams after finally being able to sleep, she hadn't actually been *able* to fall asleep until well after three in the morning and had to be up before seven to open the store at eight. She was exhausted and it was putting her on edge. Although he was a pain in the butt, she knew Ryan wasn't doing anything out of the ordinary for him and he didn't deserve to have her sniping at him.

"Sorry, boss, I'm just incredibly tired. I couldn't sleep last night and I woke up late so I didn't have time for coffee before I came in. I'll work on being more of my sunshiny self."

"Well, maybe don't go that far," Ryan said sardonically. Jordan smiled at him and his face softened. "I'm sorry, too. Being tired sucks and I know how you are with your coffee addiction. Why don't you take a fifteen and go get a jolt? I can hold down the fort until you get back."

"Really?" Jordan asked enthusiastically. "That would be great! Thank you. Do you want me to grab you anything while I'm over there?"

"Sure, I'll take a coffee. I had a somewhat late night, too, and caffeine couldn't hurt."

"Perfect, I'll be back in a few." Ryan waved her off and turned back to his computer, opening the folders.

Jordan walked back to the register, grabbed her hoodie, and walked over to the grocer's. The bite in the wind told her winter was coming in earnest to New England and their little town of Shamore would soon be snow-covered for the better part of four to five months. It didn't bother Jordan; she loved the snow. In this respect, she still felt like a kid at heart. She loved sledding, ice skating, wintery drinks like hot cocoa and apple cider, building snowmen and snow forts, and most of all, she loved reading a book by the fire with the snow falling gently outside their house's big, picture window. She managed a smile as she walked into the warmth of the store and headed back to the coffee shop.

Sawyer matched her smile when he saw her coming. "Hey," he said, looking at his watch. "I was just going to head over in about an hour or so to bring you a lunch-time beverage."

"That's sweet of you, really, but with the sleep I got last night, I couldn't wait that long. *Ryan* actually suggested I come over and get coffee, if that tells you anything."

"Wow. I think it tells me you need a triple shot for sure. Any particular flavor you're feeling, or would you like it directly in the form of an IV?"

Jordan laughed. It really was so easy to talk to him and he obviously understood her. At least, he understood her coffee needs. And that was a big part of her overall, general needs, she thought. "That'd be great, but I'm not sure the technology is quite there for intravenous coffee yet, so I'll have that triple and toss a little vanilla and cream in there for good measure and I should be good to."

"Coming right up!" Sawyer grabbed the cup and began making the drink. "So, how was your day off yesterday? Did you at least get to relax some before a night of not sleeping?"

Jordan's mind went back to yesterday. Relaxing was so the opposite of how she would describe that day. It was true, she didn't feel any desire to tell Sawyer her and Georgia's secret, nor was she afraid she would let it slip anymore. Talking about her secret with someone really seemed to tighten the lock she had on it everywhere else in her life. It also seemed to help that it wasn't only *her* secret anymore. Now, she was protecting someone else as well, and that made it all the more important. She remembered their conversation after the events of the day and felt happy all over again to finally have a true friend. She remembered what Georgia had said about Sawyer and how thoughts of him had contributed to keeping her awake so late.

"Jordan?" Ryan asked again, bringing Jordan out of her head. She saw him extending the finished drink to her with a look of mild concern on his face.

"I'm sorry," she said, taking the drink from him. "What did you say?"

"Man, you really are out of it today, huh? I'm sorry you got such crappy sleep last night. I asked if your day was at least relaxing to make up for some of it?"

"Oh. Well, it wasn't really relaxing. It was actually pretty eventful. But it ended up being a great day, so it was still worth it. Thanks for the concern." She smiled and took a drink. The warmth of the beverage flowed through her and she felt instantly better.

"Well, that's good I guess," he said, smiling back. "Would you still like me to bring another drink over on your lunch? I tend to take mine around the same time, so it's really no trouble. I wouldn't want you falling asleep in the store somewhere and have Ryan get angrier than his usual cranky self."

"Oh, thank you for reminding me! Ryan wanted a small plain coffee as well."

Sawyer's eyes widened. "Really?! I don't think I've ever seen him drink coffee before. That's new." He grabbed a small coffee cup and pumped some pre-brewed coffee into it. "Does he take any cream or sugar?"

"Um, I honestly don't know. I don't think I've ever seen him drink coffee either," Jordan laughed. "Why don't you give me a couple packets and some of those little creamer cups. I'll let him doctor it up however he wants himself."

"Good plan." Sawyer put the sugar packets and cream cups in a little bag and draped it over her arm before handing her the small coffee cup. "So… about me bringing another coffee by in an hour? Do you think you'll be ready for jolt number two?"

Jordan looked into is eyes and could see Georgia had been right. He did want to spend time with her. And more than that, she really wanted to spend time with him as well. They didn't have much interaction beyond his keeping her and her friend in coffee. She found herself wanting to know more about him; to hear more of his story. She knew she would run the risk of him asking about her as well, but she thought she might be able to come up with enough stuff to share that wouldn't jeopardize anything or anyone.

"You know, I do think I'll be ready for another coffee, but I have a different idea if you're open to it."

"Oh?" he asked, intrigue in his voice. "What's your idea?"

"Well, if you're taking your lunch at the same time as me, why don't I come back over here, and we can take our lunch together? Maybe we can grab some sandwiches from the store, sit at one of your tables, drink coffee, and chat."

Sawyer's smile was bigger than she'd ever seen before and she couldn't help the blush that rose to her cheeks as she looked down at her coffee.

"I love that idea," he said. "But can I make one minor alteration?"

"Sure. What are you thinking?"

"Well, I was thinking that, while having a meal together here sounds fantastic, maybe if we're going to do the lunch thing together, we could do it somewhere that isn't one of our work places. We could expand our horizons, as it were. The sandwiches here are great and all, but maybe we could go down to the corner restaurant and have a nicer meal there. I'm pretty sure we can still chat there and, while their coffee leaves much to be desired, it *is* still coffee." His nerves had rushed him through his speech, but he seemed proud to have gotten it out.

"I love that idea," Jordan said, grinning encouragingly. "I've had my share of bad coffee and Mama Landry's is far from the worst. Should I meet you there at one?"

Sawyer looked relieved she had been so agreeable to his plan. "I'll be outside the bookstore at ten 'til. I'll walk you down there."

"Great." Jordan turned to go. "I'll see you then," she said over her shoulder.

"Can't wait," he said, and she smiled broadly as she walked to the front door. Me either, she thought to herself.

"Here you go," she said as she walked into Ryan's office, setting the coffee and bag with the cream and sugar down in the "in" tray. "Now, I've hidden your beverage and fixin's, so if you can't find it within a few minutes, you let me know and I'll help you."

Ryan turned around and looked at the coffee and bag in his tray and gave her a mildly amused look. "Feeling more yourself, I see." He picked up the beverage and bag.

"I am!" she said. "And I have a lunch date with Sawyer, so I have to get out of here a little before one. I'll be taking my full hour today, so if you could hold things down here until I get back that'd be great."

"Sawyer?" Ryan asked, one eyebrow raised. "Is that the coffee guy from next door? I knew he'd been in here a lot lately. Do you think it's wise to date your supplier?" he gibed. "I mean, if things don't work out, where will you be able to go for decent coffee?"

Jordan was about to say something sassy back when the truth of his statement hit her. What if they had this date and it didn't work out and it was awkward and weird between them? He wouldn't want to see her all the time if that happened, so she would only be able to go to the grocer's café when he wasn't working. Or she would have to find somewhere else altogether. She was growing to love the coffee there; that would be a disaster.

"Oh, for God's sake," Ryan said, pulling her out of her thoughts. "I was just giving you a hard time. He seems like a good kid. I'm sure it'll go fine. And please don't tell me that, if for some reason it isn't a love connection, you wouldn't even be able to bring yourself to see him long enough to get the coffee you like. That's a little weaker than I pictured you being."

He was right again, she thought, sighing. She was clearly putting too much thought into this. She decided to respond maturely. She stuck out her tongue at Ryan and turned to leave.

"Hey, how much do I owe you for the coffee?" Ryan called after her.

"Nothing. He never charges Georgia and I for coffee and I guess he didn't charge for yours either."

"Hmm, now he definitely seems like a good kid," he said, pouring one of the creams into the coffee and stirring it. Jordan shook her head and made her way back to the counter.

Chapter Eight
The Date

"I'm heading out to lunch," Jordan said, poking her head through the open doorway to Ryan's office. "There's no one in here right now, so just listen for the bell. The lunch rush is done, so it shouldn't be too bad. I'll finish the orders for the week when I get back. They're almost done anyway."

"Sounds good," Ryan said. "Have a nice lunch date." Jordan pulled her hoodie over her head and opened the front door. Sawyer was waiting outside the door as promised. He smiled at her and held his arm out toward the corner restaurant. She started walking and he fell into step next to her. They walked there in silence, the brisk afternoon air blowing against them. Jordan snuck a few sideways glances at Sawyer as they walked and noticed how his shaggy, black hair lifted slightly in the breeze. He really was quite good looking, she thought to herself. Fortunately, the red blush in her cheeks was masked by the wind nipping at both of them which had already reddened their faces. They reached the door to the restaurant and Sawyer pulled it open. "After you," he said, with a slight bow. Jordan grinned and walked through with Sawyer following close behind. It looked like much of the lunch crowd had gone and there were only a few occupied tables.

"Welcome, welcome," Mama Landry said, coming out of the kitchen carrying a plate of food in each hand. She was a rotund, dark-skinned woman with short, black hair that was greying around her hairline and which she kept wrapped in a scarf. Her customary large smile was outlined by bright red lipstick with no other makeup and her patterned dress was covered by a white apron. "You sit whereva ya'd like and I'll be over in a jif."

Sawyer walked to the farthest corner booth by the window. It was the same seat Jordan would have chosen and she liked that they seemed to be on the same page fairly often. He took off his coat and put it on the booth bench against the wall and slid in after it. Jordan sat down on the bench across from him, pulling her hoodie off. It was always warm in Mama Landry's restaurant. The heat from the stoves in the kitchen seemed to make it unnecessary to turn on the regular heat, even in the middle of winter, and it gave it a cozy kind of feel. Jordan always liked it there and wondered why she didn't come more often. Probably, she thought, because she wasn't a big fan of dining out on her own. Maybe if things worked out with Sawyer, she'd be able to come more often.

"I'm starving," Sawyer said, picking up two menus from the table and handing one to Jordan, his gaze working its way over the pages of food offered. "I feel like I want one of everything."

"I'm getting there myself," she said, sending darting glances up at him every few seconds to check out what he was doing. "Um, the chicken pot pie is amazing. And her meatloaf is my dad's favorite."

"I think I'm sold on the pot pie," Sawyer said, closing his menu. "It caught my eye when I opened the menu and, if you say it's amazing, I'm going to trust you on it. So… what are you going to get?

"I'm torn. I really do love the pot pie, but spaghetti sounds amazing too." She kept her eyes on the menu.

"Well, I'm getting the pot pie," he said. "So maybe you could get the spaghetti and we could share?"

"Perfect!" Jordan said, closing her menu and setting it aside. She looked at Sawyer before she realized she was doing it and their eyes met. She quickly looked down again. Why was she so nervous, she thought? They'd had conversations a dozen times before about more riveting things than food choices and they'd been perfectly normal. Had this been a bad idea? Were they meant to be just friends, and nothing more?

She and Sawyer took it in turn to glance at each other without speaking for a while before Mama Landry broke their silence. "Well, Miss Jordan, it's been a age since you been in here. I missed seeing ya face! What can I get fo ya, sugar? Gonna have the pot pie today? I know it's one a ya favorites."

"Actually, Mama Landry, I convinced Sawyer to try it and, since he's such a smart guy, he had the great idea we could share our meals so I can order the spaghetti." Sawyer chanced looking up and met her gaze. They smiled at each other.

"One'a ya otha favorites," Mama Landry smiled. "Ain't ya a sweet young man ta accommodate this young lady's fancies? You wanna hold on ta a young man like that, child," Mama Landry winked. This time it was Sawyer's turn to blush and Jordan chuckled softly.

"Yes, ma'am, I probably should. Could you also bring us one of your famous shakes?" she looked to Sawyer again and added, "To split?" Sawyer nodded, smiling.

"I surely can, sweets. Would ya kids like anythin' ta drink?"

"Coffee," they said at the same time and all three of them smiled.

"Well, don't that beat all? Ya two young'uns sharin' the same brain waves. That's a treat ta see. I'll be back with ya food in just a few, but I'll bring out ya coffee'n shake first."

"She seems like a really nice lady," Sawyer said watching as Mama Landry walked to the kitchen.

"She's like a second mother to everyone around here. I bet she's babysat every kid in this town at one point or another, and most of their parents honestly. I probably haven't been in here in close to a year, but she still remembers my favorite dishes. She's wonderful."

"You're wonderful," Sawyer said, and then took in a sharp breath, surprised by his own boldness, and looked back at the table. Jordan looked up quickly in surprise. The compliment had come out of nowhere, but the way it made her feel was amazing. "I'm sorry if that was cheesy," he said, looking slightly embarrassed. "I've just been thinking it for a while now and felt like I needed to say it before I lost my nerve."

"That's really nice of you to say, Sawyer," Jordan said quietly, staring at her hands in front of her and nervously picking at her right thumb nail. She was sure he had just said it to be nice. She'd never had the chance to interact with people much; especially guys. She couldn't imagine what about her would seem wonderful, so she followed up with "I'm just me though… I don't know what would be wonderful about me."

Sawyer watched her for a minute and then steeled himself. He took a deep breath and proceeded quietly, but quickly. "It's true. You took on a crazy boss like Ryan and got him to go against his outdated notions of how a store should be run, and now the place is doing better than ever. You have an amazing sense of humor. You're smart. You're… beautiful." Jordan's hands stopped moving when he said this, and he cleared his throat and powered on. "You befriended a new girl in town and have been an incredibly loyal friend to her and made her feel welcome. And… and you took a chance in associating with the new guy to town even though he's the grandson of one of the most intolerable men ever."

At this, Jordan had to laugh a bit. "Auggie's not that bad," she said quietly.

Sawyer seemed to gain confidence in her not being repulsed by his comments. "Ok, sure. And no comment on your other many attributes?" Sawyer asked, taking the chance to look at her.

"Honestly," she said, taking a deep breath and fixing her eyes on him. "I guess it's just hard for me to believe you could think that. I've never had anyone want to go on a date with me before, so this is all very foreign to me. Although, the truth is, I think you're pretty wonderful as well. I was trying to pretend I didn't notice because I've always been one to distance myself from people, but with you it's just so easy to talk and have a good time. This is based off previous interactions of course. I feel like I'm being an idiot tonight." Sawyer laughed and shook his head in disagreement as she continued. "You make me feel, I don't know… safe; like I don't have to worry what you'll think of me when I say stuff. That doesn't mean I don't embarrass myself in front of you," she laughed nervously. "But it seems easier to take."

Sawyer smiled and reached across the table, taking Jordan's hand. There wasn't the cooling feeling, like when she and Georgia came in contact with each other. Instead, there was a heat that spread from her hand through her whole body. "I like you, Jordan." Sawyer said, this time not taking his gaze from her face. "I want to spend more time with you; to get to know more about each other."

"I'd like that too." Their eyes remained locked on each other.

"Here we go, darlin's. One milkshake, two straws. And here's ya coffees." She sat everything down in front of them. "Enjoy," she said with a knowing wink and walked away.

"I wish we had more than 45 minutes," Jordan said, reluctantly letting go of Sawyer's hand and picking up her straw.

"Me, too. So… when's your next day off?"

"Not until the end of the week," Jordan answered.

"How about your next free afternoon we go for a walk? If it's not too cold, we can walk around town. If it's nasty out, we can walk around the market or take up residence in a booth here and talk for hours until we're both thoroughly sick of each other."

"I can't see that happening, but I like the plan," Jordan said, beaming. Sawyer took his straw as well and they both sipped at the milkshake.

Chapter Nine
A Sadness

One Sunday morning a few weeks later Jordan woke and stared at the wood beams of her bedroom ceiling. She couldn't believe how much her life had changed in just a few weeks. She had spent a lot more time with Georgia in the woods talking for hours about the events of their past. They would often transform and run through the woods, talking and laughing, and Jordan had showed Georgia the lay of the land. Even though the weather was getting progressively colder as the New England winter set in, they could travel much farther in their animal forms and soon Georgia was almost as familiar with the area as Jordan was. Through many frequent conversations at both of their homes, it came to light that Georgia would spend time in the woods on her own when Jordan was otherwise occupied; be it working or spending the other half of her free time with Sawyer.

Jordan's face spread into a smile as she thought of Sawyer. Being with him had been so much easier than she had even imagined it could be. They had spent hours on their past few dates talking about their lives before they met, family, school, and interests. Jordan had figured they would run out of things to talk about at some point, but it hadn't happened yet. While she still had zero plans to discuss anything to do with what she and Georgia jokingly referred to as their "freaky little secret", she hadn't felt close to slipping up about any of it, even when she and Sawyer had gone for walks through the woods, which he had insisted upon. Jordan knew every inch of the woods, so she guided him along miles of outer trails, never coming anywhere remotely close to her and Georgia's secret clearing with the pond.

She had even spent some time with Georgia and Sawyer together. He would come over and spend their lunch breaks with them a couple times a week when they had shifts together. The three of them had formed a very comfortable friendship.

Jordan had also really grown to love Georgia's mom. She and Georgia had spent a few meals at each other's houses the past couple weeks. Her family had accepted Georgia immediately and conversation at the dinner table was almost as if she had a sister. They checked in on how she and her mom were doing and invited her to join them with most things, including the upcoming holiday festivities. When it came to time with Amy, it was a bit like Jordan had a second mother; one who knew her secret and could give her advice on the subject. Georgia had been telling the truth; Amy couldn't change and neither could her father. Amy had reaffirmed the fact that she simply had a friend in her youth who was able to do it and who had told her all about it and how to control it. She didn't know what caused it and couldn't offer any advice as to how to find out, but the comfort of having a mother figure who knew was nice. It had been hard watching Amy grow weaker through the passing weeks, but her attitude had always remained the same. She was pleasant and loving with a great sense of humor. Even when the evenings consisted of nothing more than the girls sitting on the floor next to the couch where Amy lay, talking about everything from books to boys, they had still been some of the greatest nights. Amy loved hearing about Jordan's blossoming relationship with Sawyer almost as much as Georgia.

Jordan brought her fingertips to her face and gently touched her lips, remembering her and Sawyer's date the previous night. Her eyes closed, and she let her memories drift back to the end of the evening. They'd had a great meal at Mama Landry's restaurant, which they decided was going to be a Saturday night ritual for them. Then Sawyer drove her back to her house where he had also picked her up that morning to bring her to work.

They sat in the car talking and laughing late into the evening. "I should really get inside soon," Jordan said reluctantly. "I'm scheduled to be at work a couple hours before opening tomorrow so I can do the new holiday setup and put away the holiday shipment that came in yesterday. I'm supposed to meet Georgia there. It's going to be a big job and Ryan wants us both there."

"I get it," Sawyer said. "I hope you have a good rest of your evening and sleep well. As much as I love seeing you and taking you to work in the mornings, you're going to be on your own getting there tomorrow. I have some work to do at the farm tomorrow, so I probably won't be in to see you guys until around lunch time, but I promise to bring you giant coffees for you to refuel."

"That'll be great. I'll see you then." She reached for the door.

"Wait," Sawyer said. Jordan stopped and turned back to face him. He reached his hand out slowly to touch her chin. She looked into his eyes as he brought his face closer to hers and kissed her gently. Heat seeped through her body as he pulled back, scanning her face to read her reaction. She smiled and leaned forward to kiss him again. She felt his smile through the kiss and then his hands were in her hair. Her hands found his face and the back of his neck. The kisses deepened and she lost track of time as the romantic tension that had been building between the two of them since they met finally bubbled over and they gave in to it. After close to ten minutes, Sawyer softened their kisses and ran his thumb over her cheek, his forehead pressed against hers. Jordan had breathed in the now familiar smell of his cologne and minty breath. "Sorry," he said on a whisper. "But I've been waiting a while to do that."

"It's a shame you waited so long," Jordan laughed and gave him another quick kiss before really opening the door and getting out. She waved from the door and he waved back before pulling away.

Surprisingly, she *had* slept well, dreaming of Sawyer and his kisses. He had given her quick pecks on the cheek and lips before, but nothing like that. Remembering it all was making it hard to get out of bed, but she knew she had to be to the store to let Georgia in. Plus, she couldn't wait to tell her all about her evening. Georgia was very invested in their story since it had been her that had encouraged Jordan to pursue him in the first place. She pushed herself up off the bed and forced herself through her morning routine. Since Sawyer had told her there would be no coffee before lunch, Jordan filled two large thermoses with her favorite blend. Sawyer had actually brought both her and Georgia a bag. She also grabbed a couple of CDs Georgia had told her she was interested in hearing so they could listen to them before the store opened. It was going to be a good day she thought to herself as she made her way to work.

Ten minutes before the store officially opened, Jordan's mood had gone from blissful to downright terrified. Georgia was supposed to have met her at the store almost two hours ago. Jordan had tried calling her several times, but there had been no answer. She had even called Sawyer and asked him to drive by her place on his way to the store when he came for lunch to see if she was home and if everything was ok. Clearly things weren't ok, she thought, or she would be here. Or at the very least, she or her mom would have answered the phone.

She made up her mind that if Georgia didn't show by the time Sawyer got there, she would have Ryan watch the store and she would leave to go look for her herself. Jordan opened the store and turned back to the register. It was a good thing she had been able to get most of the setup done and the shipment put away, because no more work would be getting done this morning, she thought. Not when she was this distracted and worried. She could barely focus on the tasks at hand. Every time the phone rang, she lunged at it, hoping to hear Georgia's voice on the other end. It was only customers, though, and Sawyer once to check in to see if Georgia had made an appearance.

Ryan came in a couple hours after the store opened. He walked to the register and gave a small wave. "Mornin'. Where's your partner in crime? She in the john or did you guys need a refuel after the early-morning start?"

"She never showed!" Jordan could tell her voice was starting to reach a hysterical pitch, but she couldn't help it. She had been keeping the cooling sensation in her chest at bay for close to two hours and it was starting to take its toll on her. Fighting a transformation hadn't been this hard in years and, even though the book store was one of her favorite places in the world, she wished she was anywhere else at the moment. "I've been calling her, but no one's answering. I asked Sawyer to drive by her place, but he won't be able to do that for a while still. I'm really starting to freak out."

Ryan's face registered genuine concern. For all the hell they gave each other, he had become fond of them, and they of him. He knew it wasn't like Georgia to not show up for a shift, or even be late for one, without letting someone know. "When was the last time you spoke to her?"

"I talked to her yesterday morning for a minute, but she never mentioned anything about possibly being late or missing the shift today. She even confirmed the time we were meeting and asked if I needed her to bring anything. She sounded fine. She was going to spend the day with…" Jordan trailed off, a thought striking her to her very core, eliminating the cooling feeling completely and replacing it with a hollow, empty feeling. "Oh, God, Ryan. You don't think…"

The bell above the door tinkled and they both looked toward it. Georgia pulled the door shut against the wind and turned to face them. Her eyes were red and puffy. Her gaze met Jordan's questioning look and her face seemed to crumple. Jordan sprinted toward her friend and caught her as she fell into her arms, sobbing. Jordan looked over Georgia's shoulders at Ryan. His eyebrows were knitted together in puzzled concern. 'Her mother' Jordan mouthed at him and understanding washed over his face and he bowed his head.

"Georgia, you didn't need to come in," Jordan said, stroking her friend's hair as she cried. "You should be at home. You could've just sent word or something."

"I c-couldn't s-stay there anym-more. I needed to g-get out. I can't…" she dissolved into sobs again.

"I get it," Jordan said understandingly. "Come on, let's get you back to the stockroom so you can sit down." They both walked her to the back room and got her seated at the table where they sometimes took their lunches. "I need to call Sawyer and let him know he doesn't need to search the town for you anymore. We've all been worried sick about you. Ryan, sit with her a minute while I call him."

"Sure," Ryan said, sitting next to Georgia and rubbing her back while she sat, her head buried in her arms, her shoulders still shaking. Jordan had never seen him be comforting before and it warmed her heart to know he cared for them as much as he did. Maybe she should start being nicer to him, she thought. She lifted the receiver to the phone in Ryan's office and dialed Sawyer's number. He answered on the second ring. "Sawyer," she said. "Georgia turned up at the shop. Her mom died. I don't know if it was late last night or this morning, but she's a wreck. Ryan and I are in the back room with her, but we've got her so no need to drive by her house."

"Oh, God," Sawyer said, the pain in his voice palpable even over the phone and even with the farm machinery running in the background. Jordan was sorry she had blurted the news out so bluntly. She knew how much Sawyer cared for Georgia and the news would, of course, be devastating to him too, especially with him having lost his parents as well.

"I'm so sorry," Jordan said. "I didn't mean to be so blunt about it. I just wanted you to know she was safe. I didn't think…"

"Jordan, it's ok. Of course, I'm devastated for her, but I'm relieved she's ok. Thanks for letting me know. I'll try to get over there as soon as I can. See you in a bit."

Jordan set the received down and took a deep breath. The day had started so great and it looked like it was going to have a rough ending, but as she walked back to the store room, she had to at least acknowledge how lucky she was to have these people in her life that all cared about each other so much. Yes, it was going to be a rough day; probably a rough couple of weeks. But they were going to get through it because they had each other.

She returned to the store room to see Georgia was sitting up and talking softly to Ryan. She couldn't tell what was being said, but after a pause in Georgia's speaking where she assumed Ryan was saying something, she saw a small smile on Georgia's face before she responded. Jordan smiled as well. She was going to be ok. It might take months; it might take years. But she was going to be ok and it was because, even though she had lost her mom, the last member of her biological family, she still had a very real family here as well and they were going to take good care of her. Jordan walked to the table and sat in the empty chair next to her friend. Georgia gave her a watery smile and leaned her head on Jordan's shoulder. Jordan put her head on Georgia's and her arm around her waist.

"I'm going to let you guys chat for a while," Ryan said, standing up. "Don't worry about the shop. I'll keep an eye on things for a while. Georgia, if you need a ride home or anywhere at any point, just let me know."

"Thanks, boss," she said, her voice wavering but stronger. He gave her a wink and walked down the hall toward the sales floor. The two girls sat in silence for a while.

"It isn't like I didn't know it was coming," Georgia said finally. "I just thought I had a little more time. I think she must've known though. She made so many plans for this week. Now that I think about it, it was probably just to keep my mind off things; distract me from how bad it was getting. She was so thin... so weak." A small sob escaped her throat and she took a shaking breath. "I just really don't want to go back to the house yet. I had to call Doc Wilson to come take her. That was hard enough. I know I'll have to go back at some point, but I don't want to be alone right now."

"Then you won't be." Jordan said decisively, moving her arm up around her shoulders. "You'll sit back here as long as you like. Sawyer's coming at lunch with coffee. And after we close, you'll come home with me and stay as long as you like. I'll even go to your place and pack you an overnight bag if you want."

Georgia's eyes filled with tears again and she turned and hugged Jordan tightly. The cooling feeling was a comfort for both of them. "I keep thinking she was the last person I had and that now I'll be alone, but it's not true. I'm so lucky to have come here and met you and Sawyer and even Ryan. I know I'll be ok; it's just going to take some time."

"Of course it is! And you take as much of it as you need. We're all here for you. Can I ask something? If you're ok to talk about it, I mean. If you want to wait, that's totally understandable."

"No, it's fine. Honestly, talking helps."

"Well, now that it's just you in the house, are you going to be able to afford to stay there on your own with just the wages from the bookstore? I mean, I know your mom was splitting things with you."

"She left me enough that I should be ok for a while. I could get a roommate I suppose. Or I could move somewhere smaller. I hadn't really thought about it. I didn't want to..." she trailed off.

"I'm sorry. I shouldn't have brought it up," Jordan said guiltily.

"It's really ok, Jordan," Georgia said a little stronger. "It's a reasonable question and one I really should think about. Just because I *can* afford to live there on my own doesn't mean it's the best financial choice. Maybe in a few days when I'm feeling more up to it I'll look around to see what's out there. It's not like it's a big town," she grinned.

Jordan couldn't believe how brave Georgia was being. She may have had time to prepare for this, but if it had been her mother, she didn't think she'd be handling it nearly as well.

"I had a thought," Jordan said timidly. "I'd have to run it by my parents, but you've been in my room before. It's the whole attic of the house so it would be more than big enough for a second bed in there. If they're ok with it, do you think you might want to move in with us for a while? I'm sure they'd ask next to nothing in rent if they'd even accept anything at all, and it'd give you a chance to save and add to what your mom left you. If you plan to stay around town, maybe you could get up enough to put a good down payment on your own place after a while."

Georgia's eyes widened. "Do you really think that's something Judy and Gordon would consider?"

"Well, you've been around enough the past couple months that I think they're starting to consider you part of the family anyway," Jordan laughed. "They adore you. It's worth checking into if you're interested."

"That would seriously be amazing. I already consider you a sister and they've been like another set of parents since I moved here; this would make it even more real."

"It's settled then," Jordan said, standing up as the bell above the front door tinkled for the third time within a few minutes. "We'll go to my place tonight after closing and ask them. If for whatever reason they say no, who knows, maybe I'll just come live with you!"

"Either one of those sounds perfect. Go on and help Ryan. I'm sure with more than two people in the store he's beside himself. I'll be ok back here for a while."

Jordan slowly walked to the door of the stock room. "If you need someone, call us. I don't care how busy it is, one of us will come back here."

"I swear, I'm fine for now. And Sawyer will be here soon. Thank you so much for being you, Jordan. I'm so grateful to have you in my life."

"Me too, sister," Jordan smiled and walked up to the sales floor to help Ryan.

Chapter Ten
In Memoriam

In the days that followed, Georgia was surrounded by support and love. Jordan hadn't been surprised when her parents had okayed Georgia to move in with them for as long as she needed. She planned to hold on to the house she and her mother had lived in through the next few months until the six-month lease they signed and prepaid was up. Then she would move in with Jordan and begin her new life on her own; but not alone.

The day of Amy's funeral dawned bright and cold. It was only a couple weeks until Christmas, but the weather had been unusually mild for the time of year. Christmas had always been one of Georgia and her mom's favorite times of year and, though she was sad it would be the first one they wouldn't be spending together, it still held some of that holiday cheer for her which helped her get through it all.

Even though they were essentially "new" to the town, quite a few people remembered Amy from her years there before, and more had come to care strongly for Georgia, so there was a very respectable turnout for the service and the burial. Amy had left instructions with Georgia to have it be a fast and light process, and her wishes were granted. After the burial, many people went back to the corner restaurant where Mama Landry and some of the other ladies from town had organized a potluck to celebrate Amy's life. Everyone visited and ate until they were stuffed. Slowly, people filtered out and eventually it was just Georgia, Jordan, and Sawyer left in the booth they always shared. One side of the booth was piled high with Tupperware containers full of casseroles and desserts as well as bags of other miscellaneous gifts. The three of them sat together on the other bench of the booth with Georgia in the middle. They had positioned themselves this way the entire day, flanking her and protecting her. From what, they really didn't know, but she appreciated their friendship and support in getting her through the day.

"I think you did really well," Sawyer said, rubbing one of her shoulders. "I know this was a really hard day for you, but you handled it like a champ. I bet your mom's looking down on you so happy with how you got things taken care of for her."

"Thanks," Georgia smiled weakly. "It was definitely a rough day, but it would've been unbearable without you two. You got me through it and I'm thankful to you for that. I'm just relieved it's done and I can try to start moving on and healing. Next chapter, you know?"

"Absolutely, forward but never forgotten." Jordan agreed, her arm resting on Georgia's other shoulder. "Do you want to stay at our house tonight, or do you want me to come to your place?"

"Actually," Georgia said, leaning her head back against the wood of the booth behind her, "I think I want to spend this evening alone at my place." Jordan's eyebrows raised as if asking if she was sure. "I think I need to just have this evening with her spirit in the place that was ours. I need to say goodbye that way."

"No problem," Jordan said. "If you change your mind or things get too hard, you know where to find me and how to reach me."

"And me," Sawyer added.

"I do," Georgia said. "Jordan, do you want to meet at our place tomorrow around one? I was thinking of spending some time there since it's starting to get a bit colder and we might not have many more opportunities until spring."
"Absolutely," Jordan agreed. "I was thinking that myself."

"Am I ever going to be let in on the location of this secret place?" Sawyer asked, feigning hurt at not being included.

"I like you a lot," Jordan said, putting her hand on his which was still on Georgia's shoulder. "But, no."

All three of them laughed and Sawyer scooted out of the booth first so the girls could follow. "Fine," he said. "It's a girl, bestie, sisterhood thing. I can accept that. You're just lucky I'm so well adjusted."

"I tell myself that every day," Jordan laughed, brushing her lips across his. "And it doesn't hurt that you're cute, too."

"Ugh, don't get gross on me now," Georgia groaned and Jordan laughed.

"And she's on the mend!"

"Hey, Mama Landry," Sawyer said as the woman pushed open the swinging door to the kitchen and stepped through it. "How much do we owe you? We're going to head out I think."

"Not a dime, sugar. This one's on Mama Landry." She came over and gave Georgia a tender hug. "Ya mama was always a real sweet lady and I'm sure glad ta see so much o'her in ya. You gonna continue ta make her proud, I know that's a fact. If ya ever wanna talk 'bout her, or 'bout anything at'all, you come talk ta me. Ya take care now, sweets. Go getcha some rest and don't be a stranga now, ya' hear?"

"Yes ma'am," Georgia smiled, hugging her back tightly. "Thank you so much for everything you've done today, and every day."

"Don't ya give it another thought," Mama Landry said, waving them off. "Bye, now. See y'all soon, I'm sure. G'night darlin's."

They all walked single file out the door into the cool, night air. "She's such a sweet lady," Georgia said, turning to face the other two. "I want to spend some one-on-one time with her one of these days and see if she has some stories about mom from before I was born."

"That's a great idea! I bet she has a lot of them. She's known everyone in town for decades!" Jordan said. "You could find out all kinds of things you probably never knew about her."

Georgia nodded and pulled her keys from her pocket. "Anyway, I think I'm going to head out. Thank you both again for everything today." She hugged Sawyer. "And I'll see you tomorrow," she said to Jordan as she hugged her next.

"You sure will," Jordan said, squeezing her best friend tightly. "Mama Landry was right. Try to get some rest tonight." Georgia nodded and walked off toward her car.

Sawyer's fingers weaved into Jordan's and they stood on the sidewalk, watching Georgia drive off toward her house.

"I hope she's ok tonight," Jordan said, resting her head against Sawyer's shoulder.

"I think she will be. But why don't I get you home now just in case she wants to call. You should be by the phone." Jordan turned and put her arms around his neck and kissed him gently. His arms wrapped around her waist and pulled her closer to him.

"You really are an amazingly sensitive and sweet guy; you know that?" Jordan said, breaking their kiss and looking into his eyes.

"You make it easy to be," he answered. "I'd do anything to make you happy."

"That works out well, because you make me very happy with just about everything you do." Jordan rested her forehead against his chest. "I can't believe how lucky I am you came into my life; our lives."

"I'm the lucky one," Sawyer whispered and rested his chin on top of her head. "I love you, Jordan."

Jordan lifted her head so quickly Sawyer's jerked up as well and he bit his tongue in surprise. "Ow," he said, laughing a little and raising his hand to his mouth.

"Oh my god, I'm so sorry," she said, reaching up and touching his face. "You just… shocked me. What did you just say?!"

Sawyer moved his hands down her shoulders, gripping her arms lightly. He pressed his lips together, trying to stifle his smile. "I said 'I love you, Jordan.'"

Jordan had never imagined hearing those words from anyone other than her parents. The feeling was completely foreign and, at the same time, incredible. Her heart felt as though if it got any bigger, it would burst out of her chest. Looking into his eyes, she could tell he didn't *need* her to say anything back. How he felt about her wasn't dependent on how she felt; he was simply sharing his feelings with her. And he loved her. She didn't need any time to think about how to respond, however. Her face broke into a wide smile. "That's what I thought you said, but I almost couldn't believe it. I love you, too. So much." His smile matched hers and he brought his lips down to meet hers once again. They stayed that way for a few minutes before Sawyer pulled away and pushed a loose strand of her hair behind her ear.

"Come on, let's get you home by that phone in case your friend needs you. I'll call you tomorrow to make plans for the week." He took her hand and walked her to his car. He held open her door while she got in and he closed it behind her. As he drove her home, Jordan couldn't help staring at him. He was so genuine in his feelings for her.

He always tried to make sure she was taken care of and happy. He anticipated her needs in a way that felt almost like he was in her head, and yet, even though she had always been a loner, this sudden influx of attention didn't crowd her like she'd been afraid it would. On the contrary, it seemed to fill a void she had never even known she had.

And there was Georgia. He treated Georgia with such kindness and respect. He was never jealous of the time they wanted to spend together, and he respected their privacy when they asked for it. He was truly something special. Between the two of them, Jordan didn't think she could have asked for better people to surround herself with.

She didn't even realize they had made it back to her house until she felt the car shut off and heard Sawyer's voice say "I hope you guys have an amazing time tomorrow." She came out of her thoughts and looked at him. "You've been awful quiet the whole way home. Are you ok?" He asked, looking slightly concerned.

"I'm beyond ok," she answered reassuringly. "I've just been thinking about how different this year would be playing out if you and Georgia hadn't come around. I mean, it's terrible about Amy, but I bet Georgia's handling it better than she would've on her own. And you're a big part of that."

"You're a bigger part," Sawyer said, winding a lock of Jordan's hair between his fingers.

"Shush, it's my turn to say nice things about you."

"I'm sorry, go on," he laughed.

"You're a big part of how amazing Georgia is handling things. You've been there to support her. You helped her with the funeral arrangements, which couldn't have been easy for you and had to bring back terrible memories. You helped us move and sell a lot of their stuff. You stored all the extras of the food people brought over. You found a home for the flowers that wouldn't fit in the house. You've been going non-stop ever since this happened on top of your job at the coffee place *and* working Auggie's farm." She paused here and took his hand from her hair and held it in hers. "And you've really made things easier for me as well. I've been really focused on Georgia lately and you haven't complained once. You've been more than understanding and I don't know how to show you just how much I appreciate that. I'll spend a long time trying to make it up to you."

Sawyer grinned. "While I like the sound of that, there's no need for you to make anything up to me. Things have been busy at the farm since our new farm boy quit last week and I've had to pick up some slack there, so I've been forced to give you two more time than I'd normally want to," he joked. "But seriously, anything I do, I do because I care about you; and Georgia. You need to be together now. I'll get my time with you, too. Hopefully a lot of it. I've been through what she's going through and it's hard. Friends and family are important and we're all she has right now. It's just human decency to be understanding and supportive. Full disclosure though… my gramps *did* eat one of her casseroles before I could stop him."

They both erupted into laughter. Jordan laughed harder than she had in weeks; the stress of the past few days melting out of her. When they finally stopped and were still for a bit, Jordan took a deep breath and said, "I should get inside. I want to be there if she needs me and I need to get some sleep. She and I are going to spend the day together tomorrow, but I'd love to see you after my shift on Monday. Are you going to be available, or do you have to work on the farm?"

"Monday afternoon I'm all yours," Sawyer said, leaning over to kiss her. Jordan soaked in the warmth from his lips and then gently broke it off.

"I really do love you," she whispered.

Sawyer grinned, "You sound surprised about it."

Jordan smiled and leaned back. "It honestly is surprising to me. Not that I love you; that part is easy to believe. It's just surprising that I'm able to connect with anyone enough to let myself love them. I've spent so much of my life avoiding people so I wouldn't get close to anyone because I thought it was the best and safest decision. Now I see what I've been missing."

"I still don't get that," Sawyer said, shaking his head. "How could depriving people of your amazing heart and mind be the best and safest decision for anyone?"

"Just trust me that I believed it to be true for a reason. But we don't have to worry about it anymore. I think it's safe to say I'm close to you!"

"I'm looking forward to getting even closer," Sawyer growled seductively and kissed her yet again. Jordan tolerated it for a few more minutes and then grabbed a hold of the door handle.

"You're going to make me not want to get in there and I need to. Save your thoughts for Monday and we can revisit them then." She winked and got out of the car, shutting the door behind her and waving as she walked toward her door. Sawyer waved back and, when she opened the front door to her house, he pulled away into the darkness. She watched him until she could no longer see his tail lights and then went inside, closing the door behind her. She sighed contentedly. In a way, she felt a little guilty for being so happy at a time when her best friend was feeling so badly, but she knew Georgia supported her and Sawyer's relationship and wanted her to be happy. As she headed toward her room to get ready for bed, she resolved to help make her friend happier tomorrow as well.

Chapter Eleven
Bedtime Stories

The following afternoon found Jordan sitting crossed-legged on the bank of the pond, watching the swan swim lazily around. It seemed like the last few times she and Georgia had met in their spot, the swan had shown up to spend time with them as well. It stayed on the opposite side from where they visited for the most part, but today it almost seemed to sense something had happened and was closer than usual. Jordan felt comforted by its presence.

A soft rustling in the distant shrubbery alerted her to Georgia's impending arrival. She looked over her shoulder as Georgia approached, sat down across from her, and crossed her legs to match Jordan's. They both watched the swan for a while before either spoke.

"So, how was your evening?" Jordan asked, turning her eyes from the swan to face her friend. "Did you get any sleep at all?"

"I did, actually." Georgia responded, turning as well so they were face to face, their knees almost touching. "It was good I had an evening alone with her memory. I looked through our picture albums. I pulled the last of the cookie dough we made together last week out of the freezer and ended up eating fresh baked cookies and milk for supper while I sat in her favorite chair and remembered all the bedtime stories she told me over the years. It was almost like she was right there with me and I eventually fell into a very good sleep. I didn't wake up once until this morning.

I actually feel… good." She finished, sounding surprised at her own choice of words.

"Georgia, that's great!" Jordan said, reaching out and touching her friend's knee. "I'm so glad you rested and had that chance at some closure with your mom's spirit. I've never been particularly religious, but I absolutely believe in life energy and I bet your mom's was definitely with you last night." They sat in comfortable silence again for a bit before Jordan spoke again. "Did you say bedtime stories?"

Georgia laughed. "Yeah. Well, I guess it was really more like one incredibly long story. She started it when I was about six or seven and she just kept building on it. Of course, it's been a while since the last installment, but I still remember almost all of it. I think it's why I love fantasy books so much. The right ones remind me of that story and of her. Even when she was alive, I loved the feeling they gave me of having her around. I have a feeling it'll be even more so now."

"That's so cool! My mom always read me stories when I was younger too, but she never made one up for me; especially one that spanned years!" She paused. "Maybe you should try to write some of it down. Who knows, you could end up writing a book we could sell in the store. Oh, you could dedicate it to your mom; maybe even name it after her or something!"

Georgia didn't say anything for a while. She looked as though she was thinking about what Jordan had suggested. Finally, she responded. "I suppose I could try. I've never written anything other than assignments and papers for school. The stories in our house were always just spoken, ya know? It was a story she made up just for me to fit my situation. I kind of like that it was just between her and me."

"I can absolutely respect that. It was just an idea. It'd just be so neat to know someone who wrote a book we sell in our store. You don't have to share it with the world if you don't want to but... would you mind sharing the story with me? Or at least what you remember of it? Maybe doing that will make it fresh again and you could even pick up where she left off." That idea seemed to please Georgia. Jordan leaned over so she was lying on her side with her arm bent and her head resting on her hand and waited for Georgia to begin.

"Well... she always said it all started thousands of years ago in a place that was just like where we lived at the time, only older, obviously. The country was far less populated then and was made up of just a few dozen families and their descendants. But each of those families had special gifts; gifts of magic. Some of them practiced alchemy and potion making, some were telekinetic, some could read minds, others could see the future, and so on. These gifts were passed down through the bloodlines to all the descendants of that family. But my favorites were the ones she called shapeshifters. They were the ones who were like me; like us! They could change their shape into animals at will.

The two biggest and most powerful families were shapeshifting families, and they were the only shapeshifters in existence. They were called the Onirus and the Nephiryon families. There was no technical hierarchy at the time; no one was king or queen or president or prime minister or any of that, but all the families knew the Onirus and the Nephiryons were the most powerful. Since magic of the human mind, like telekinesis, was practiced by the human magic families that possessed those powers, they only affected other humans. Shapeshifters weren't susceptible to those kinds of magic because they weren't entirely human. They could be affected by potions, poisons, and other alchemy-based magic, but it often didn't affect them as strongly or in the same way as it did humans.

The patriarch of the Onirus family was named Bernard. He was a good man who advocated peace and cooperation among the land. While he knew he was exceptionally powerful, he never used his powers against anyone unless it was out of self-defense or protection. He believed every family brought something of value to the table and he had appreciation for everyone.

The patriarch of the Nephiryon family was Edmund. He was *not* a good man. He believed the ranks of power existed for a reason. He advocated the development of a hierarchy based on the level of power each family had. He agreed with Bernard that each family had something to contribute, but his selfishness made him believe those things should be contributed to the service of the most powerful families. After a period of time, it became apparent he wasn't going to succeed in his plan through the proper channels and he became angry the others in the land didn't seem to agree with him enough to support his cause. His anger led him to begin taking actions into his own hands through more sinister channels. He began to recruit people of specific powers to bring into his service using bribery, manipulation, and threats. If someone crossed him badly enough or refused to do his bidding, he'd strip them of their power."

"How could he do that?" Jordan broke in, clearly enthralled by the story.

"Well, by that point, he had many powerful people in his service. A large number of them were alchemists and potion makers. Some were spell casters. They found a way to combine their powers in such a way they were able to strip someone of their power forever. If magic was powerful on its own, it could become even more so when combined with another.

Anyway, Edmund eventually made so many enemies he began a full-on war. His goal escalated from only wanting certain magic at his service, to actually eradicating the land of all magic unless it served him or was deemed useful in his eyes. He called on Bernard Onirus and his family to join him as the only other family of the 'highest power' as he put it. But Bernard couldn't bear to stand by and watch Edmund destroy these people's gifts, so, despite his hatred of conflict and violence, he chose instead to fight against him.

The war raged on for many years. Edmund's numbers were smaller since most feared him or had already been stripped of their magic. Bernard had the loyalty of the masses that remained, including those who had already been stripped of their power. But he was unpracticed and less skilled in the art of war than Edmund. And, his remaining alchemists and potion makers, though loyal and desperate to help him, couldn't find a way to stop

Edmund's ability to destroy magic, nor could they determine a way to bring magic back once it had gone. Slowly, Edmund stripped almost all the people in the land of their magic and thousands of them were killed in the process.

"So, if Bernard had the numbers but Edmund had the seemingly unstoppable power, how could anyone win?" Jordan asked, anxiously.

"It was hard to tell who really had the upper hand at any given point. But Edmund was no fool. He knew with the way things were playing out, the war would inevitably leave him with little to possibly *no* masters of magic to choose from to rebuild his army when it came his time to rule. You see, Edmund was a very arrogant man and, though his intelligence told him the war would have to end with him and Bernard coming face to face in a final battle, he never paused to think of what might happen if he were to *lose* that battle. So, he called on his subjects to create a token; a token like nothing that had ever been attempted before. The purpose of the token would be to use it to recruit others that weren't born of magic to serve him by giving them magic abilities; *his* magic abilities. It'd give them the ability to shapeshift and, therefore, give them the highest form of power. He wanted something he could keep with him at all times and that could be easily hidden, so his subjects fashioned him an amulet. A part of him was needed to complete the magic of the amulet, so inside it, they put some of Edmund's blood. Edmund believed blood to be the most powerful material because it was how magic was passed down. Not to mention, he considered himself the most powerful man in the world, so his blood would make the amulet the most powerful object to do his recruiting.

Fortunately, Bernard was also a smart man. He called on his most trusted followers to help him create a token as well. Bernard's intentions were purer than Edmund's and, as he wasn't so arrogant as to assume victory like Edmund, the purpose of his token went beyond the current conflict. Bernard wanted the token to exist, not to win the battle, not to serve his own personal purpose, and not to gain control of the land, but so that some semblance of good, pure magic would always exist and, therefore, evil could never truly rule the world. So, he asked his loyal followers to leave the war efforts and work tirelessly to fashion him the token. Work they did, and finally, they too crafted an amulet into which they placed some of Bernard's tears. Bernard knew that, while it was blood that carried their magical power, tears came from a place deeper than even blood ran. They came from the collected workings of the heart, mind, and soul. Tears could be shed in moments of happiness as well as sadness, and those two emotions encompassed all a person could be."

"That's amazing! So, two opposing forces created the same token but for completely different reasons." Jordan said in awe.

"Yep. Then, finally, with the help of his multitude of supporters, Bernard was able to infiltrate Edmund's hiding place."

"How could Bernard find Edmund if he had so many of the best magic people hiding him?"

"Well, Bernard played to Edmund's weaknesses. As I said before, Bernard valued all people, even after they'd lost their magic. Edmund already thought people who were of 'lesser' magic classes weren't as powerful. Can you imagine what he thought of people who had *no* power?"

"He probably thought they weren't even worth noticing... oh!" Jordan said, understanding setting in.

"Exactly," Georgia nodded, grinning. "So, by using people who were completely under Edmund's radar, he was able to find where Edmund was hiding. Once he was in, he confronted Edmund. Bernard tried to assuage Edmund's anger and get him to see reason, but by this time, Edmund's thirst for power had consumed him. They battled fiercely, and both were greatly wounded. Edmund swung his sword at Bernard, cutting his chest deep and severing the chain that held his amulet, which fell to the floor and shattered to pieces. In deep despair and desperation, Bernard lunged, running his sword through Edmund's stomach, dealing him what would ultimately be a fatal blow. As he watched the light slowly leaving Edmund's eyes, some of his soldiers entered the room, saw his wounds, and took Bernard to get medical attention. One of the soldiers, however, noticed the broken amulet on the ground. He picked up what remained of it and took it home to his wife who was a maid in the Onirus house. They swore to each other to keep it hidden and safe in the hopes that some of its power had remained and Bernard's wish for good, pure magic to always exist in the world, no matter what was to happen in the war, could be fulfilled.

Bernard survived his injuries, but the cost of the war weighed heavily on his heart. He was so devastated at the magnitude of magical losses and the families that were torn apart that he chose to henceforth never use his magic again. In an act of solidarity, his followers all followed suite and so, after many years and generations, magic eventually left this world."

"What about Edmund's descendants?" Jordan asked.

"Mom never really had anything to say about them other than Edmund didn't have any children of his own. He was too busy focusing on himself and his cause to think about things like carrying on his lineage I guess. If the stories were actually true, it would be likely that, once Edmund was gone, most of the people who were serving him would'e been happy to have their freedom and probably stopped pursuing his cause.

Mom usually ended the story by saying the descendants of the Onirus and Nephiryon families almost certainly still had magic dormant in their blood, but that's why no one today believes magic really exists. It was too much for humanity to be able to have such power, and Bernard wanted to save the world from another war of that magnitude."

Jordan stared out over the water as Georgia's story ended. The swan, who seemed to have been listening to their story, had gotten closer than it ever had before. Both girls looked at it and it looked back at them. Finally, Jordan looked to Georgia and smiled. "God, wouldn't it be amazing if all of that *were* actually true? You could be a descendant of Bernard Onirus. That'd explain your abilities."

Georgia rolled her eyes and stood up. "Mom made up that story so I wouldn't feel bad about being different. She knew if she made it sound like my ability to change came from something good and pure I'd feel better about it; less like a freak. She was an amazing woman and I love her for it. The truth is, you and I, we're just anomalies. And that's ok."

"I guess," Jordan said, leaning back onto the ground and looking up through the trees. "But wouldn't it be great to be more than just an anomaly? I mean, you and I could be sisters if it was all about bloodlines."

"Or we could just as likely be descendant from mortal enemy families," Georgia laughed. "There were two families, remember? Actually," she paused and looked thoughtful. "I never really thought about it, but I could technically just as easily have been from the Nephiryon line as the Onirus line. I guess it shows I like to see the good in myself that I never thought that before." They both smiled. "Besides," she held her hand out to Jordan, who took it, and pulled herself up to a standing position. "I think of you as a sister anyway; blood or no blood."

They hugged and turned back to the pond one more time. They both jumped as they saw the swan had come all the way to their bank and was less than two feet away from them.

"It's been getting closer the whole time," Jordan whispered, staring at the swan. "It must be getting used to us. It seems interested anyway."

Georgia reached her hand out toward the swan and took a few tentative steps toward it. The swan held its place for a moment, then started to slowly float away from them.

"Give it more time," Georgia said, retracting her hand. "Maybe it'll decide to join us one of these days." She and Jordan turned and began their walk back to Jordan's place for supper.

Chapter Twelve
Unease

"This doesn't make any sense," Jordan muttered, looking through the shelf at the store where they kept special orders, her brow furrowed.

"It's really early on a Monday for things to not be making sense," Ryan said, emerging from the hallway to his office. "What's got you confused?"

"Our orders shelf is fuller than I've ever seen it. I'm running out of room to put the arrivals."

"Ok, is this an elaborate, looking-for-compliments type of thing? Yes, I get it. Your idea was a good one. More fantasy books, younger crowd to draw in, so many orders the shelf is now full, blah, blah, blah. I've told you already your plan worked out well. I'm not going to keep feeding your ego."

"What?" Jordan said, breaking her focus on the shelf and looking at Ryan in confusion. "Oh! No!" Jordan said in exasperation. "I mean, yes, it was a good idea, but no, that's not what I'm talking about. We have twenty-six orders on the shelf, twenty-two of them came in at least a week and a half ago, and *all* those twenty-two have had two notification calls placed. It's like no one is coming in to get their merchandise for some reason."

"Well, all the orders are prepaid, so it's no skin off my rear. I guess if they don't pick them up in another week or so, we can document them and reshelf them. If they want to come in after that, we can sell them what's on the shelf if it's still there, or we can order them another copy and just have them pay the shipping again. This isn't a bad situation," Ryan said, looking at Jordan with one eyebrow raised, trying to understand her annoyance. "Just leave them for another week and we'll see what happens. There are a couple empty shelves in the stock room you can use if you run out of room up here. Listen, I need to run to the bank to do a deposit and then I'm going to do a couple other errands. You hold down the fort and I'll be back before your shift's over."

Jordan gave him a small wave, still looking at the inventory list for the order shelf, her brow still knitted. Ryan shook his head and the tinkle of the bell above the door followed him out.

Why was no one coming to pick up their orders, thought Jordan? Ryan was right; the orders had all already been paid for. But that made it seem even odder. Why pay the money and never come get what you paid for? She couldn't remember ever having had this issue before. She reviewed the names of the people who had made the orders. John Lewys, Angie Raynolds, Mark Onus, Patty Shiff, Joleen Schadt, Brad Merus, Dale Neff… the list went on. They were all people she knew, not that that was saying much since the town was small and everyone knew everyone else, but these were almost exclusively adults from their late 40s to late 50s. She knew this because a number of them were parents of people she'd gone to school with. She searched through her memory trying to think of the last time she'd seen any of the people on the list. Had any of them been at Amy's funeral? She thought hard and reread the names over and over again. She couldn't remember seeing any of the twenty-two names with outstanding pick-ups at the funeral. A few of the kids of some of the people had made it, but not a single name on the sheet had been there.

The bell above the door tinkled again and Jordan slid the list under the register before raising her head to greet her customer. She was surprised to see Mama Landry walk into the store.

"Mama Landry!" Jordan said, smiling. "I can't remember the last time I saw you outside the restaurant and I don't think you've ever been in here to see me before. I'm glad you got a chance to get out of there for a bit; you deserve a break. Can I help you find anything?"

"Good mornin', sugar," Mama Landry said, pulling her scarf away from her face. "I'm here ta pick up a cookbook I ordered. Mr. Ryan called me yestaday ta tell me it was in."

"Absolutely," Jordan said, pulling the book off the orders shelf and setting it on the counter. "I'm just glad *someone's* coming to pick up their stuff." She realized she had said it a little more bitterly than she meant to and gave Mama Landry an apologetic look. "I'm sorry, Mama Landry. It's just been a confusing and frustrating morning. Did you want to look around at any other cook books before you check out? Or is there anything else you'd like to look at I might be able to help you find?"

"Oh, that's ok sweet pea." Mama Landry's voice was kind but had a hint of concern. "Let Mama Landry lend you her ear ta bend if it might ease ya worried lil' heart. Did ya say no one's comin' ta pick up they orders?"

"I'm sure I'm just being silly," Jordan said, leaning forward onto the counter. "We have over twenty orders from the past two weeks that people haven't picked up. We've called them all twice, so they have to know it's here. And with Christmas coming, it's likely a lot of these are gifts. But it's like they paid for the items and then just changed their minds or don't want to come in for some reason. I don't know. And I can't remember seeing any of them at the funeral or even around town lately. It's bizarre. I know I'm probably worrying over nothing, but I can't get it out of my mind that something's fishy about it all."

"Honey, I know what ya mean." Mama Landry stood looking at Jordan but not saying anything. Jordan didn't know if it was her imagination, but it almost seemed like Mama Landry was trying to decide whether she should say anything further. She knew it wasn't her imagination, though, when she saw the resolve in the woman's eyes set in, and her gaze met Jordan's with intensity as she went on. "I've had a number'a holiday orders for pies and meals not show up at the restaurant too. Seems like these past few weeks, people's been actin' less like theyselves. Some o'them ain't comin' inta town at all no more. In fact, a few'a my regulars been missing in action for weeks. S'definitely fishy like ya say."

"Really?" Jordan felt her senses tingling. So, something definitely wasn't right around town, but there wasn't much to go on except for people flaking on orders. "If I showed you my order list, could you tell me if some of the people on my list are people that've bailed on orders for you, too?

And can you tell me if you've seen any of these people around town recently?" She handed her order list to Mama Landry who took it and read slowly. The further she read, the stonier her face became.

"There's four people on here have orders at the restaurant they ain't picked up. I don't reckon I seen any of these folks 'round town, but Mr. Onus and Mr. Neff live down my end of town and I seen them getting in they trucks and drivin' off late at night a couple night these past few weeks. It struck me as odd at the time 'cause they both work second shift at the mill, and I think they been going ta work as well, so late evening's usually time they come get settled at home. They seem ta go ta work and go do whatever it is they doing late at night; they just ain't been coming inta town lately." She paused holding the order list and stared off into space over Jordan's shoulder.

Jordan glanced over her shoulder to see if Mama Landry was looking at anything in particular, but there was nothing behind her except the wall with a few pictures of town landmarks; the church, the courthouse, and the mill among them. "Mama?" Jordan said tentatively.

Mama Landry blinked and focused her eyes back on Jordan. She handed the order list back to her and her tone suddenly got lighter and a bit more rushed as she said, "Ya might not wanna worry much 'bout it, sugar. I'm sho it's just coincidence. Ain't that many people in this town; it prolly just seems more significant than it really is. After the holidays, things tend ta calm down and get back to normal."

Jordan looked hard at Mama Landry's face to try to read whether she believed what she was saying or what could have caused her shift in the way she was speaking, but the woman wouldn't make eye contact with her any longer. She couldn't be sure, but now it seemed like Mama Landry was trying to warn her away from the topic. But why would she do that? Jordan forced a smile and picked up the cookbook from the counter. "You're probably right. I've just been stressed and tired with the funeral and all of that."

"And I'm sure them late nights with ya gentleman friend don't help none neither," Mama Landry said, winking at Jordan and grinning.

Jordan blushed and smiled back at Mama Landry. "Oh yeah, that too. Sawyer's a great guy. He's been such a help these past few weeks."

"He definitely a sweet young man. And comin' from the same stock as cranky ol' Augustus Toole, it's a wonder he ain't mean as a snake and twice as slimy," Mama Landry laughed. "Ya fortunate ta have the affections of sucha good young man."

"I am," Jordan nodded in agreement. "So, just the cookbook for you today?"

"That be all, sweets. Thank ya so much for gettin' that in so quick for me. You three young'uns should stop in sometime next week. I'm gonna be makin' up a new soup; a gumbo matter a'fact. I think you'll love it."

"Sounds great! I'll talk to them and we'll make a plan for sure." She took the cash from Mama Landry's hands, rang up the book, and handed over her bag and change. She watched the woman walk toward the door. Just as she reached for the handle, it was opened from the other side by Georgia.

"Well, if it ain't another ray'a sunshine on this cold and gloomy day. Hi there, sugar. How ya feelin' today?"

"I'm doing really well, Mama Landry," Georgia said, letting her squeeze her cheek gently. "Are you picking up a book today?"

"I am. Miss Jordan already got me what I needed. I told her she had ta get you'n Mr. Sawyer ta come visit Mama Landry next week and try my new gumbo recipe I'm workin' on."

"Oooh, I love gumbo! Mom and I used to eat it back home all the time. I can't wait to try yours. I bet it'll be even better. Everything you make is amazing."

"You's a sweet girl," Mama Landry said, reaching out and giving her hand an affectionate squeeze before reaching for the door handle. "I'll be seein' ya three later. Ya'll stop in any time." She looked back at Jordan before saying "Don't be strangers now," with a pointed look and then walked out, shutting the door behind her.

Georgia gave Jordan a questioning look and walked to the counter. "What was that about?"

Jordan motioned Georgia to come closer and lowered her voice, even though there was no one else in the store to hear them. "There's something weird going on around here, and I think Mama Landry knows something about it. We have over twenty orders that are pre-paid, yet haven't been picked up, even after two calls. Some of the same people not picking up their orders here haven't picked up their holiday orders at the restaurant either. I haven't seen any of these people in town lately and Mama Landry hasn't either. Plus, she's seen a couple of them going out late at night even though they worked late shifts at the mill already and should be in bed."

Georgia's eyes widened a bit as she looked at the list. "You know, I did think it was weird I had to make a second call on a couple of these since they'd been so excited for their orders, but I didn't put nearly all that together. I guess I'm not as familiar with everyone yet. But I did actually just run into Brad and Angie the other night." She pointed to their names on the list. "I was taking out the garbage super late and they just happened to be walking down the street. I let them know I'd made a second call to them about their orders that came in and we were looking forward to them picking them up. Both of them brushed me off, kind of rudely actually, and left in a hurry. I thought it was weird because Brad's actually been pretty flirty in the past," Georgia paused. "So, you're saying all the people on this list haven't been seen around town, aren't picking up any of their stuff, and, in Brad's case, they're acting differently?"

"Basically, yes," Jordan answered. "Plus, think about all the people who have been either quitting their jobs or not showing up to them. It's like the town's gone crazy."

"Well, that does seem kind of bizarre, but couldn't it just be the season? I mean, Christmas stresses everyone out at some point, right? Or it could just be coincidence. It stands to reason that if someone didn't pick up their order here, whatever the reason was keeping them from that could've also prevented them from picking up their order at the restaurant."

"I guess…" Jordan conceded. "But, the attitude changes, unreliability, and the weird nocturnal activity makes me wonder if something else is going on."

"Like what?" Georgia asked, bemused.

"Well, Mama Landry said two of the men on here that live by her work second-shift mill jobs. I'm looking at this list and, of the people on here who I actually know where they work, all of them work at the mill. I'm almost willing to bet a couple of them are also delivery drivers…" she trailed off and paused a minute before looking at Georgia and continuing. "Is that still just coincidence? Suddenly, a large number of people that work at the mill have become stressed by the holidays and are thereby unreliable and surly as well as have begun participating in late-night travels after their long, stress-filled work days?"

Georgia looked at the paper for a long while before responding. "Yeah, ok, that all seems a little unlikely. But what is it you think is happening if it's not coincidental? What do you want to see happen here? I mean, other than the obvious answer of people coming in to get their books and pies and to start being more generally reliable and pleasant to each other?"

"I know you're mocking me, but I'm going to ignore it because what I want is information!" Jordan exclaimed. "I want to know what's happening to make these people not come into town anymore. I want to know where they're going so late at night and why. And I want to know why it seems to be predominately affecting people at the mill."

"Ok, ok." Georgia said in a calming manner, putting her hands up in front of her. "I didn't mean to upset you. I was trying to keep things light because I can see you're agitated. Why don't we do some asking around town? We can put a bug in some people's ears; people who can be trusted to not read too much into it."

"That could work," Jordan said, still pouring over the list.

"Yeah, and we can talk about it in the woods this afternoon if you'd like. We're supposed to have a cold snap starting tomorrow and I don't see an end in sight. We may have a lot fewer days to spend time in the woods until spring. We can talk over what we want to say and ask and go from there." She reached out and took the list from Jordan, sliding it under the register.

"Ok," Jordan agreed with a sigh. "Thanks for not thinking I'm completely crazy and for helping me with this."

"Oh, I still think you're crazy." She laughed and Jordan gave her a mock scathing look. "But, you've been amazing with helping me through this thing with my mom and I'm going to help you through this now because that's what friends do. And don't worry, you're not *completely* crazy. You're just a little crazy." She pulled her friend into a quick hug over the counter then reached past her and grabbed a bag from under the register, holding it up to Jordan. "I came in to grab these books I bought the other day but left here on accident. I plan to do some reading by the fire when I get home and then I'll see you by the pond late afternoon, yes?"

"Yes," Jordan said, finally smiling.

"Good. Try to have a decent rest of your day. Don't stress. We'll figure out a plan tonight."

"Thanks, Georgia." They both waved as Georgia closed the door. Jordan looked down at the list under the register and pushed it even further back. Georgia was right. Nothing was going to be accomplished by worrying about it now. She would just get through the rest of the day and then be able to talk it all out in their spot after work. Jordan squared her shoulders and went to the sales floor to straighten the shelves so she wouldn't have to stay later than necessary.

Chapter Thirteen
Secret Exposed

Jordan ran out to her car the second Ryan told her she could go. Despite her attempts to not think about the weirdness going on in town, it was pretty much *all* she had thought about. She was all but convinced the key to whatever was happening had to do with the mill, but she had no idea what could be going on to cause the issues.

She got into her car and tore off to her house. She couldn't wait to get to the pond to brainstorm with Georgia. They had to find a way to get information from someone at the mill. She considered transforming at the edge of the woods and running to the pond. Even though she hadn't lost much of her human speed since graduating, she was definitely much faster as an animal. Still, she knew it wasn't worth the risk of someone being on the trails on the edge of town and witnessing her change, so she went inside to grab her boots and then took off on foot to the middle of the woods. It had been rainy the past few days and her feet made squishing sounds as they pounded through the mud.

She finally crashed through the bushes into the clearing and looked around. Her breath fogged from her mouth and nose in white clouds. A quick scan of the area told her she had beaten Georgia there, so she sat on the downed tree near the edge of the pond and caught her breath. The ruckus she made upon her arrival had caught the attention of the swan who had come out from behind the willow curtain to glide toward her. She watched it for a while until she heard a distant rustling behind her announcing Georgia's arrival.

"Sorry if I'm a little late," Georgia said, stumbling through the bushes at the edge of their clearing. "This mud is ridiculous. It was like walking through sand that refused to let go. I think my jeans are wet all the way up to my knees and the mud goes almost as far. I was so close to just changing and running that way."

"Me, too," Jordan said. "But there are enough people still walking on the trails I figured I didn't want to risk it."

"Same here," Georgia said, sitting opposite Jordan on the log and kicking her feet against the bottom of it trying to get the extra mud off her shoes. "I'm almost ready for the snow. At least it's less messy. You still get wet but drying is easier than chipping yourself free."

"Yeah, snow is much easier," Jordan agreed dismissively. "Anyway, I've been thinking about the town weirdness and I have an idea."

"Getting right to it, I see. OK, go," she said, crossing her arms to keep warm.

"I still feel like our answers are at the mill. Maybe we need to ask around; see if anyone else has noticed the absence of a lot of the mill workers in town. We also might need to find someone to talk to who works at the mill to see what's been going on there. If something changed, it might help us figure out the issue."

"All right. Do you have any idea as to whose help we should be enlisting?"

"I'm having trouble with that particular detail. As you know, I wasn't that close to the people from high school, so the few people I know who went to work at the mill right afterward really aren't an option. They'd probably ask a lot of questions."

"Starting with 'Hey, haven't seen you since graduation. Why are you asking all these really weird questions about things at the mill?'" Georgia asked.

"Something like that," Jordan replied. "I thought maybe we could lean on Mama Landry again, but after I got the information from her this afternoon about the two mill workers at her end of town, she locked down and would only talk about Sawyer and gumbo," she said, frustrated.

"Do your parents know anyone we might be able to ask?"

"I don't think so. Unfortunately, the thing I'm proudest of about them is also what's hindering their involvement in this process. Since they didn't go into the typical jobs around town, they didn't make a lot of friends in those fields either. The only people dad really talks to are former police. As a police officer, he's met and interacted with just about everyone, but he patrolled the other end of town mostly so any calls for the mill would've gone to the other officers. Mom knows a lot of the same kids I do since she worked at the public library as well as part-time in the library at my school, but she didn't get close to many of them because, well, teachers getting overly friendly with the students is frowned upon."

"Understood," Georgia nodded. "Would Ryan know anyone?"

"He's more into befriending the business people around town, not the laborers. I guess we could ask him, though, if we can't think of anyone else. Couldn't hurt to have him as a backup."

"Ok, and what kinds of things are you going to ask or have him or someone else ask exactly?" Georgia questioned.

"I really just want to know if it's only coincidence that the majority of the twenty-two people on our list also aren't picking up books and food, or if the issue is more widespread. I want to know if it's everyone at the mill that's becoming more unreliable and reclusive, or just a few of them. I'd also like to know if anyone has seen any changes at the mill that might make these people act this way. I figure it could be something like layoffs are being threatened and that would make people hold on to their money in case they might be losing their jobs. It would also mean their bad moods could be justified. *And* it could mean people are working extra to either prove their dedication or get more hours to get more money, again in anticipation of potentially losing their jobs."

"That's good thinking," Georgia nodded. "I almost wish this was happening back in my old town. If something was going on with one of the businesses, that news would have leaked to the entire town by the end of the day. This place may be a small town, but the gossip chain is not well developed at all."

"It's always been that way. People support each other when needed but keep to themselves most other times. It seemed like a positive thing when I was growing up, but it's inconvenient right now. Still, if we find the right person or couple of people to get on our side, we might be able to get the info we need. So, what I think we should do is brainstorm a list of people we can potentially ask and then reconvene to decide who the best candidates are and how to approach them."

"Agreed," Georgia said. "Are you feeling better about it at all? We have a plan and soon we'll have questions to ask and people to ask them to."

"I do actually. Thanks for catering to my craziness. I know it probably doesn't make sense to you, but the book store patrons are my people and this town is my town and when things aren't right, it gets to me."

"I totally understand. I think it's one of the wonderful things about you. You really care about the wellbeing of the people here. It's a good thing; not crazy at all." Georgia stood and swung her arms to try to get her blood flowing again. "Would you mind if we reconvened somewhere warmer next time? Maybe back at your place or next to my fire place?" She looked over at the swan who had been floating right against the bank closest to them the whole time they had talked. "I don't know how that poor thing can stand it. That pond can't be more than a couple degrees from freezing solid. I know Sawyer said he had to fill the barn water troughs at least twice a day the past few days because the ones out in the fields were freezing over already."

"Oh my god!" Jordan exclaimed. Georgia jumped, and the swan flapped her wings in alarm. "I totally forgot about Sawyer! We made plans to meet after my shift today, but I was so wigged out about this whole thing and getting here to plan things out with you that I completely forgot. He's going to think something's wrong. I need to get back home fast and call him... or find him... or something."

"Oh, no! Poor guy. Ok, so why don't we change now, run until we're about half a mile from the edge of the woods behind your house, and then we can change back and circle around until we hit the trail that goes close to your driveway? We can listen really well before we change back to make sure no one's around and we should be safe. Plus, it's getting pretty dark now so the likelihood of anyone being out is slim and if they *are* out, they'd never be able to see us when the woods are still that thick. Sound like a plan?"

The swan squawked from the pond and flapped its wings again. Both girls looked at it and then turned to face each other. "I guess it agrees with your plan." Jordan shrugged. "Let's do it. I don't want him to be worried sick."

The moved a little farther apart from each other and took deep breaths in, concentrating on the cooling feeling inside. Jordan was stressed enough about missing her date with Sawyer that the change came easily to her. Shortly after her completed change, she heard the front paws of her best friend hit the ground next to her. She opened her eyes and looked to Georgia who was in her bobcat form just to her right.

"Ok, let's head south. It shouldn't take us long to get there." They both swung around to run away from the pond, but froze in place, never getting the chance to take a single step. Standing just at the edge of the clearing, his face frozen in a combination of shock and horror, was Sawyer. Jordan's heart stopped, and she heard the sharp intake of breath from Georgia next to her. He had seen them. She could tell by the look on his face he had seen everything. Her mind went completely blank. She knew she should be thinking of something to do; changing back to explain, running away, something. But she was frozen. She cut her eyes to the side looking to see what Georgia was doing, but her face seemed just as blank as Jordan's felt.

"What do we do?" she heard Georgia whisper low in her throat.

"Jordan? Georgia?" Sawyer finally said, in a much higher tone than his normal voice. He took a step backward, his back hitting the bushes he had just pushed through. "What the hell is going on?"

"Sawyer, I know this has to look insane, but please just stay calm and we'll explain everything." Jordan had said all this before remembering that, in her current form, he wouldn't be able to understand her. In fact, her words meant to comfort him had come out in her wolf "voice", which was a combination between a growl and a bark and, judging by his reaction, had sounded more menacing than anything else. Sawyer swore loudly, turned around, and ran back the way he had come.

"Oh, God," Jordan said, spinning toward Georgia. "We have to catch up to him. He's running blindly through these woods. He's going to fall and hurt himself, or worse, draw the attention of something far less friendly than us.

"But we'll never be able to get him to stop like this," Georgia said, her voice panicked.

"I don't know if we can catch him if we change back. I'm fast, but in this mud, he might have the edge on me. Plus, if we encounter something as our regular selves, we have no hope of protecting him."

"You should run along with your friend as you are now. When you reach the edge of the woods, change yourselves back and do your best to calm him then."

The voice that said these words was one they had never heard before and they whipped their heads around to find the source. There was no one in the clearing and they looked at each other in confusion.

'Who…" Georgia started but was interrupted.

"It is I you heard. Here, in the pond." They looked to the pond again and saw the swan, floating still at the bank where they had left it. "I know you are dealing with much in the way of surprise this evening, but please fear not. I am nothing and no one to be alarmed by. My name is Victoria and I am another just like yourselves. I am not a threat to you. Please, go after your friend. Keep him safe. Ease his mind if you can. I will not divulge your secret should anyone happen upon this place, though you are the only people I have ever seen since I came to live here long ago. I should like you to return when you have settled your affairs. I believe we have much to discuss. Good luck to you both." With this final statement, she turned and swam slowly away until the willow curtain hid her from view.

Jordan and Georgia looked at each other one final time before wordlessly deciding to follow Victoria's instructions. They would flank Sawyer while he ran until he made it to the edge of the woods and then try their best to explain the unexplainable to him. They bounded off in the direction he had run. They had the advantages of a deep familiarity with the woods combined with their heightened senses as well as their speed and they soon caught up to him as he blundered his way back toward Jordan's house.

"He's veering too far West," Jordan barked to Georgia, who was running parallel to her on her left. "Push him my way and I'll keep him from going too far East. If we keep him between us we can guide him right into my back yard."

"Perfect. We can change at the wood line and approach him normally. That'll be less intimidating." She veered farther to the left to position herself next to him and guide him back toward Jordan.

"That is if he doesn't have a heart attack first," Jordan growled and accelerated as well to be next to Sawyer on the right side. They guided him by staying out of sight. He could hear the sound of them running in the darkness, and this had the affect they wanted. He pushed away from the sound of them running and raced ahead. Jordan knew he had to be terrified and confused. She was terrified as well. He had seen them and he was trying to get away from them so intensely. But at the same time, she couldn't help but admire his strength. He moved through the woods powerfully and fairly gracefully, despite the mud, darkness, and not being on a clear-cut path. He wasn't completely falling apart but staying focused in his direction; his survival instincts strong. She was impressed. She just hoped he would be able to calm himself enough to listen to reason when they got where they were going, and they were approaching that destination quickly.

A few minutes later, Jordan and Georgia both saw some lights through the trees and knew they were approaching Jordan's house. "Ok, I think here is good!" Jordan called, and they both slowed to a stop as Sawyer continued. They were both breathing heavily from their run, but they tried to slow their breathing enough to steady themselves and transform back. It took close to fifteen seconds before they were able to calm themselves and complete their transformation.

"Jordan, I think you should go ahead and talk to him. Both of us going will just overwhelm him. When he sees you like he's used to seeing you, he might be able to calm down enough to hear you." She saw the look of panic and desperation in Jordan's eyes and rushed on. "I'm not leaving! I'll go sit on your front stoop and wait for a while. If you can't get him to stop and listen, I'll try to stop him there." Georgia's voice was soft but firm. "He loves you, Jordan. He *will* listen to you, eventually. Just give him time to soak it in and try to stay calm yourself." She squeezed her friend's arm and then made her way toward the trail that would lead her to Jordan's front yard.

Jordan looked after her for a moment as she walked away and then she took off at a jog following Sawyer through the path he had cleared while running. I really hope he loves me as much as he says he does, she thought. That was about the only thing she could think of that would be able to get them through this.

Chapter Fourteen
An Explanation

Jordan caught up to Sawyer as he reached the gate next to her house and realize the latch was on the opposite side. He whirled around and saw her approaching. He backed up against the gate and looked frantically to either side, trying to find some way to get away from her. It broke her heart to see him struggling so hard to not be near her.

"Sawyer, please wait," she said quietly, her hands up in a calming manner. "I know you've got to be absolutely terrified right now, and I don't expect you to believe me right away, but there's nothing to be scared of here."

"Nothing to be scared of?!" Sawyer yelled, his voice at least two registers higher than usual. "I just saw my girlfriend and her best friend turn into animals!"

This time it was Jordan's head that whipped back and forth, checking to see if anyone was out and within earshot. She was incredibly thankful her parents weren't home. "Sawyer, shhh, please stop yelling," she said in an urgent whisper. "Someone's going to hear you. No one knows about me and Georgia and our... what we can do. I know you probably think you're crazy or that we're monsters or... well, I guess I don't know exactly what you're thinking, but I'm betting it's something along those lines. But listen to me. I promise you we are *not* monsters and you are *not* crazy. If you'll just calm down a bit and let me at least try to explain this to you, you'll see that it's going to be ok."

Sawyer laughed almost hysterically. "Oh, it is? It's going to be ok? You just turned into an enormous dog, but I'm supposed to be totally fine with that, right? No big deal!" He turned and tried shaking the gate open before spinning back to face her, obviously not thrilled with the idea of having his back to her for any length of time.

Jordan lowered her hands, tears forming in her eyes. He was in a complete panic; his mind completely closed to anything she was saying. How was she going to be able to get anything through to him when he was like this? She took a couple of steps back, wrapped her arms around herself in the cold, and felt completely defeated. Her voice was quiet when she said softly, "You told me I was wonderful… remember? You told me you liked me and wanted to get to know everything about me. You told me you *loved* me. Well… as strange and unbelievable as it may be, this is just another part of me. It isn't something I can change; it's just who I am. I didn't ask for it." Her voice wavered as she continued. "This is exactly why I told you I never wanted to get close to anyone before; why me staying isolated was best for everyone. I was afraid they'd find out and react… well, like you are." She squatted down, wrapped her arms around her legs, leaned back so she was sitting, and rested her chin on her knee. "Then I met you. I was scared to let my guard down, but I cared enough about you that I took a chance and let myself get close to you; let myself fall for you. And now…" her voice broke and she took deep breaths trying to steady herself. She lowered her head and pressed her forehead to her knee, burying her face.

Her ears picked up the sound of the wind in the trees around the perimeter of her yard and the combination of soft sobs and quick breaths escaping her throat. Then, ever so quietly, she picked up the tentative sounds of Sawyers steps. She wiped her face on her jeans and raised her gaze slowly. He had moved toward her a few steps, but was stopped, staring at her as if unsure of what he wanted to do. She didn't say anything; just let the tears fall slowly from her eyes while he took the time to make up his mind. Finally, he took a shaky, deep breath and came a couple more steps closer to her, squatting down slowly until his eyes were at her level, almost as if he were trying to see inside of her to determine if the monster was still there.

She kept his gaze, but didn't say anything. The tear tracks on her cheeks burned ice cold in the frigid air, but she didn't wipe them away. She didn't know if he was going to stay or bolt. The look in his eyes told her he didn't know himself. He finally broke their gaze, shook his head, and gave an exasperated sigh. She blinked again and sniffed.

"I've got to be out of my damn mind," he said, almost under his breath. He stood again and crossed his arms over his chest. Defensive, she thought. She watched him but didn't stand. She figured if he was debating whether or not to run, her staying still might make him feel more comfortable; safer. The fact he would feel anything *but* safe with her gave her a sick feeling in her stomach. "Ok, fine," he said in resignation. "Go ahead and tell me how I have nothing to worry about and how this is completely fine and normal."

Jordan sighed heavily. "Sawyer, there's nothing normal about this. I never said it was normal. But I wasn't kidding when I said you had nothing to be scared of. I don't know why I can do this; why we can do this," she said, her eyes drifting toward the fence where she knew Georgia was waiting close by, "but we aren't monsters. We are our same selves no matter which form we're in. We ran with you the entire way here tonight, so we could keep you safe from any real dangers in those woods; bears or any other animals you might have attracted with your noise. If we were dangerous, we could've caught you at any point back there. But we just wanted you to be safe." Sawyer shifted but didn't retreat so she continued. "I don't blame you for being weirded out by this, but it doesn't change who I am. I'm still the same person I was yesterday and the day before that. I'm still the same person who loves you." Her voice caught here, but she pressed on. "I'm so sorry you had to find out about this; especially *how* you found out about this." She stopped here and put her forehead back on her knee. She didn't know what else to say to him. She felt like she was doing a bad job of making their case, but she'd never had to explain this to anyone before. The silence stretched so long she wasn't sure he hadn't left and she just didn't hear him go.

Then she heard the rustling of grass a couple feet in front of her and looked up to see him lowering himself to sit cross legged on the ground, facing her. She finally wiped her eyes and face with the back of her hand and watched him. His eyes had softened and weren't so wide with panic. They looked almost like the eyes of the guy she had spent the last few months falling in love with.

"I don't know how I'm supposed to deal with this," he finally said. "It can't be real. It's like I'm in a bad dream. This stuff doesn't happen in real life."

"I felt the same way the first time it happened. I spent a long time trying to wake up, but I never did. This has been my reality for over two thirds of my life. I had to learn to accept it and deal with it, too, but I've had time. Do you think..." she stopped, the fear she felt seemed to make the words stick in her throat.

"Do I think what, Jordan? Do I think I can learn to accept and deal with the fact that my girlfriend is part dog?!" He blew out a hard breath and didn't continue.

"I'm not part dog!" Jordan exclaimed angrily, and Sawyer jumped. Tears welled in her eyes again. "I am a person who can transform into the shape of a *wolf*. I'm not part of both all the time. I'm not a freak and I'm not a monster! I am who I've always been. I'm the same girl you said you loved and who you said such wonderful and amazing things about; things I had a hard time believing anyone would ever see. And I'm asking you to please try to practice some measure of understanding that this is actually difficult for me too. I'm sitting here faced with the very real possibility of losing someone I love, the first person I've *ever* loved other than my own family, because of something I can't even control. Do you know how painful that is; how unfair that is?!"

He looked at her, and his shoulders relaxed ever so slightly. "I'm sorry," he said quietly. "I guess it makes sense this is hard on you too, but Jordan, you can't expect me to just be ok with this after twenty minutes. This is insane. This is beyond the realm of believability. I'm going to need time to wrap my head around this."

Jordan nodded. "I understand that. I just… Sawyer, can you please at least promise me one thing? Whether you decide you can deal with this or not, please promise me you won't tell another soul about it? If anyone ever found out about what we can do, things could get very bad for us. There could be horrible testing, asylums, any number of awful things and my parents would never understand. Please… if you still care about me or Georgia *at all*, please keep this to yourself."

"No one knows at all? Not even your parents?" Sawyer asked, his eyes wide again.

"Georgia's mom knew. My parents have no idea. Georgia's been able to change ever since she was born. I've only been able to do it since I was ten." She told him a very condensed version of her first change all those years ago when she encountered the bear. "I didn't think they'd believe me if I told them what I could do, and if I showed them, I was afraid it would scare them enough to give them a heart attack or something. Plus, I figured they'd make me see a shrink or a doctor, I don't know." Jordan shrugged. "It's just been so long now I don't really think about it anymore. They're better off… happier… not knowing. Everyone probably is, seeing how well you're taking it all. But I learned how to control it on my own and it's just how my life is now."

"So, what about tonight? What made you… change… tonight?" Sawyer asked.

"I met Georgia in our spot in the woods; that clearing you found us in. We were talking about some weird things that're going on around town. I've been fixated on it all day and I couldn't put it out of my mind, so when Georgia came in the store today to pick up some books she left, I talked to her about it. She saw I was really worried and suggested we meet after I got off work, so we did. After we talked it through and I felt better about it all, I remembered you and I had agreed to meet. I was so upset at having forgotten and I figured you'd be worried something bad had happened, so we agreed to change so we could get to my house faster and I could call you to tell you what happened. That's when you saw us."

Sawyer shook his head and looked down at the ground. "I *was* worried. I thought something must've happened. I called your house, Georgia's house, and the book store. No one answered anywhere so I came to your house. No one was home, but I saw footprints leaving your yard and going into the woods, so I figured they were yours since you said you spend a lot of time in there. I got really worried you'd gone in for a walk and maybe got hurt or something, so I followed them."

"I'm impressed," Jordan said. "I purposely never take the regular trails, so being able to follow my footprints through the mud and brush all the way to us had to be a tough thing to do. I keep it tough to follow me for a reason," she trailed off.

Sawyer laughed softly. Jordan jerked her head up at the sound. It was like music to her ears and a good sign he was relaxing enough to laugh, though she knew she was far from in the clear with him. She kept quiet and let him continue processing.

"Jordan," he finally said, tentatively. "I'm still really freaked out by this."

She nodded. "I know. I don't blame you."

"But I also really don't want to lose you," he continued.

Her hand twitched and she wanted so badly to reach out and take his, but she stopped herself. She didn't want to scare him more or press her luck. Her voice was shaky as she replied, "I really don't want to lose you either."

Sawyer looked at her face and the single tear that had escaped her left eye. He reached out slowly and cupped her cheek, brushing the tear away gently with his thumb. "Well, at least we agree on that," he sighed. Jordan tilted her head so her cheek was firmly against his hand.

"I was scared you'd never touch me again," she whispered.

"I must be crazy, but I can't stop myself from wanting to. Even with the insanity of all this, I can't stop… loving you." He stood up and held out his hand. She took it and he pulled her up and into a soft hug. She buried her face in his neck and her shoulders shook as she cried, all the adrenaline of the day seeming to leave her at once. He stroked her hair and held her until she got herself together and pulled her face back to look at him.

"Do you want to come inside?" she sniffed. "We can have something warm to drink and you can ask me anything you want. I'll tell you anything you want to know about all this, or at least anything I actually know the answer to. Some of it's still a big question mark for me; Georgia too."

"Ok," Sawyer said, taking her hand and walking toward the back door of her house. "Let's talk it out."

"Hey, Jordan, do you want me to head out now?" Georgia called through the fence. Her voice sounded relieved. She must've heard at least part of their conversation, Jordan thought. She looked at Sawyer.

"Why don't you join us inside," Sawyer called back to her. "I might have a few questions for you too, weirdo."

Georgia laughed. "I'll meet you at the front door."

Jordan opened the back door and held it open for Sawyer to walk through. "Thank you for giving me a chance."

"I still haven't completely accepted all of this," Sawyer said. "But, I'm not willing to give you up without a fight. Even if the fight's with myself." He planted a gentle kiss on top of her head and walked toward the kitchen.

"Fair enough," Jordan smiled and followed him in.

Jordan and Georgia spent hours that evening answering all the questions they could that Sawyer asked about their abilities. They couldn't answer when he asked how it was possible or whether it was genetic, but they did their best with everything else. At the end of the night, he seemed to be less intimidated and terrified of the whole situation, but he asked for some time to think about things. They told him to take as much time as he needed, and it was almost a week before Jordan heard from him again. It had been one of the longest weeks of her life. She felt like there was a good chance they could work through it when he had left that night, but after days of no contact she started to doubt that feeling. Finally, he called her and asked her to take him out to the woods the following day to show him the whole process again in the daylight. He said he wanted to experience it again having all the knowledge they provided him and after he had time to think things through.

"Are you sure about this?" Jordan asked uncertainly. She took him into the woods; not as far as her clearing, but far enough in she felt confident no one would come across them. The wind made it bitterly cold, and anyone who wanted to go for a walk certainly wouldn't take a long one.

Sawyer swallowed hard and sat on a large tree stump. "I'm sure. I need to see it again. I need to try to work through it to be ok with it. It's just a part of you, and I love you. I need to see it again," he repeated, and Jordan could see him steeling himself.

She nodded and walked a few more paces away from him then turned around. "Are you ready?"

Sawyer gripped his knees tightly and nodded. Jordan closed her eyes and harnessed the cool feeling inside her. She felt it spread through her and out to her hands and feet, which twisted and molded into paws. She felt the front two hit the ground and opened her eyes. Sawyer's face had gone white as a sheet, but he was still sitting there staring at her. She decided not to approach him, but instead laid down on the leaf-strewn forest floor and put her head between her front paws. She couldn't think of a more submissive position to be in, short of rolling onto her side and exposing her throat, but that didn't seem to have a very "human" significance, so she went with the lying down approach.

Sawyer watched her for a bit and then slowly stood and walked toward her. He stopped a foot away and paused again. Jordan took a chance and wagged her tail slightly. Sawyer exhaled and ran his hands through his hair, smiling ever so slightly. He squatted down and looked into her face. His eyes met hers and, while she couldn't voice her thoughts to him, she hoped he felt what she was feeling. She felt the same toward him now that she always had, and that was proof enough to her that her feelings for him transcended form. She desperately hoped he felt the connection as well.

"It really is you in there, isn't it?" He said softly. She huffed out a breath and raised her head. "Right, I know you can't talk to me right now, but you said you can still understand me." He reached out and cautiously touched her shoulder. "It feels just as smooth as your hair. And those eyes," he smiled a full smile this time. "They're the same blue... beautiful." He stood suddenly and turned around. Jordan stood up as well but held her ground. "Jordan, this is crazy," he said, exasperated. "I feel like it's you, but at the same time, I mean... I'm looking at a wolf for God's sake!" He turned around again to face her, and she sat back on her haunches and hung her head. "It's not your fault," he went on quickly. "I'm not blaming you. I'm just sorting through it all. It's really jumbled." He walked back until he was standing next to her and placed his hand on her head. She leaned into him and nudged his stomach with her nose."

"I'm glad you're still being affectionate while I'm sorting through the mess in my head." He patted her and walked back to the stump to sit down. "Ok, come back to me."

Jordan closed her eyes again and a few seconds later she was standing in front of Sawyer, her human self once more. "So, did this do what you hoped it would? Do you feel better about it, or more confused than ever?" she asked gently.

He took a minute to respond, and when he did he reached out and took both of her hands in his. "I feel better about it actually. It helps me to know that, while the whole thing's incredibly hard to believe, it's definitely you either way." He pulled her down onto his lap. "I very much prefer you this way, though," he laughed and hugged her.

"Me too," she said, hugging him back. She looked up at his face and, as his dark, brown eyes looked into her blue ones, he leaned forward and kissed her. The familiar warmth rushed through her and she knew that, while they had their obstacles to work through, their connection was still strong, and she believed in her heart it would be enough to get them through anything now.

"Come on," he said, shifting her weight so he could stand. She stood with him. He put his arm around her waist and steered her back the way they had come. "Let's go back to your place and you can tell me about this weirdness you've noticed around town."

"Oh my gosh, I completely forgot about that!" she exclaimed. "I guess I had other things on my mind."

"Really? Me, too!" Sawyer laughed. "But I think we could use a change of topic for a while, don't you?"

"I couldn't agree more," Jordan said.

"Great, so call Georgia, get her over here, and we'll talk about this town mystery."

Chapter Fifteen
Victoria's Revelation

"So, basically, that's what we know," Jordan said, having just finished her and Georgia's explanation of the store's order list, Mama Landry's abandoned orders, and the odd activities and interactions of the workers they had come across recently; specifically, their evasiveness, rudeness, and the late-night trips.

Sawyer sat at Jordan's kitchen table, moving his water bottle from hand to hand, taking it all in. "You know, I wouldn't have noticed it on my own if we hadn't had this conversation, but there are a few of our farm orders that never got picked up as well. Mr. Neff never came for his cheese curds he gets every month. And Mr. Merus asked if we could save a quarter side of beef the next time we butchered. We did that two weeks ago and I've called him twice, but he still hasn't responded or gotten back to me. I think there are a couple other orders I have set back that I'm waiting to hear from people on, too.

"Those are two of the people on my list!" Jordan said, in response to the names he provided. "And Mama Landry said Mr. Neff was one of the men who's been going somewhere late at night after having worked a full second shift already. She seemed to think it was really abnormal behavior for him."

"You know, separately, these things wouldn't really mean much of anything. But I agree with you that all these things combined seem really odd. And the fact that almost all of the people have something to do with the mill; well, that's definitely somewhere we need to investigate. You know, gramps used to work at that mill. He's been retired for over thirty years, but he might have some insights into some of this. We should check with him."

"We?" Jordan asked, raising her eyebrows and looking at Georgia who shook her head vigorously. "Oh, no. I'll say hi to him if he's in town and I pass by him, and I helped him order some books a few years ago to update some of his machinery at the farm, but there's no way I'm going to go to his house and chat him up about weird goings on at the mill, no matter *how* badly I want to know."

"Ok, so by 'we' I was actually thinking me," Sawyer laughed. "I get along with him pretty well honestly, so if he'll talk to anyone about it, it might be me."

"Oh, good." Jordan said on an exhale.

"Yeah, that'd be great, Sawyer," Georgia agreed. "What kinds of things do you think we should ask him?"

"I think we should keep it simple and broad to start out with. If he's forthcoming with information, I can get more specific at that point," Sawyer answered.

"That's a good plan. Maybe you can start with something like what it was like to work there. Then you can ask him about who ran, it and how they ran it, how people were treated…that kind of thing."

"Those are good starter questions. They seem pretty benign; like I'm just making small talk. Not exactly his favorite activity, but I can be chatty sometimes, so I don't think it'd trigger any suspicions. If you're ok with it, I can judge where to go based on his answers and dig as deep as I can."

"I completely trust your judgement," Jordan nodded.

"Ok, so that's one concrete plan we have to work on figuring this out. Do you have any other ideas of what you'd like to try?" Sawyer asked.

"We discussed finding someone who works at the mill but who doesn't seem to be afflicted with odd behavior, irritability, and who hasn't disappeared off the face of the Earth. But we aren't really friendly with anyone like that what with Georgia being new and me not having gotten close to anyone because of, well… you know."

"Your furry, little secret?" Sawyer inflected, and Georgia let out a bark of laughter and quickly covered her mouth to suppress it in deference to her friend.

"Sure, we'll go with that," Jordan said, smiling.

"I haven't really gotten to know anyone around here yet either, but I could always see if they need part-time help in the mill. You told me they are always hiring and taking applications. If I got hired on, we'd have a mole in the place. I could get all kinds of information."

Jordan and Georgia stared at him for a bit. "Do you really think you could?" Georgia asked.

"Well, I've been told I'm pretty desirable," Sawyer said slyly.

Jordan shoved his shoulder and got up, grabbing her and Georgia's cups for a refill of coffee. "Yeah, yeah, you're a real piece of work, that's for sure," she said. "But honestly, if you could get in and get some deep info, that could be amazingly helpful. Why don't we see what Auggie has to say before you go taking on a third job, though? I'd still like to be able to spend *some* time with you, ya know?"

Sawyer got up, pushed his chair in, and walked to the sink, stopping behind Jordan and putting an arm around her waist. "I want that too," he said, kissing her on top of her head and setting his empty water bottle on the counter. "It's getting late and I should get going. I still need to do the final check on the cows before I head to bed. I'll try to get some time with gramps tomorrow and see what I can find out from him. We can reconvene in a few days and I'll let you know what I find out."

Jordan looked up at him and he bent down and kissed her gently. "Thank you for being amazing," Jordan said quietly.

"Yeah, Sawyer," Georgia agreed from the table. "This can't have been an easy few days for you. You've taken it better than I ever would've imagined. You really are a great guy."

Sawyer stopped in the doorway of the kitchen. "Yeah, I'm a saint. You can't imagine the kinds of dreams I've been having the past few nights. I'm looking forward to getting back to the dreams I was having before." He winked at Jordan, gave a big smile, and walked toward the front door. "G'nite, ladies," his voice called from the hallway.

"Good night," they both called after him. They listened to his footsteps as he walked down the hall, opened the door, and shut it behind him. They heard the engine of his car catch, and the crunch of the gravel as he drove away.

Jordan let out a huge sigh and leaned on the sink. "He's going to be ok," Georgia said consolingly. "He did amazing, really. The fact that he wanted to know more about it and to see it happened again today instead of dismissing it shows he's got a really open mind."

"I'm just so sorry he had to find out that way. I should've told him earlier. I was being selfish. Things were going so well and I didn't want to have a difficult conversation, but it just ended up makings thing so much worse than they had to be."

"It's over now," Georgia said, standing up from the table and walking over to stand next to her friend. "He knows and he's processing. You did great with him showing him what he wanted and answering all his questions." She grabbed the coffee pot and poured another cup for herself. "It may not have been the exact time you wanted to do it, but I don't think it went as bad as it feels to you. Honestly, if you tried to just tell him you could do something like that and he hadn't actually seen it with his own eyes, I think he would've been more likely to not believe you and bolt. Now he knows it's true, he's been able to deal with it, and he clearly still loves you and wants to be with you. Plus, now he's going to help with your concerns with the town and the mill. Things are good."

"I suppose that's true. I'm glad he's going to talk to Auggie. That man has been alive forever. He has to know something about all of this."

"I hope so. And you know what we have to do now, don't you?"

"Yeah," Jordan said reluctantly, taking her new cup of coffee back to the table. "This past week or so has been like a crazy dream. What in the world do you think that swan could possibly have to tell us?!"

"She's been listening to us talk to each other for months. It could be anything," Georgia shrugged.

"Wednesday morning?" Jordan asked.

Georgia nodded, "Wednesday morning."

"Great. I'll meet you there before work and hopefully it doesn't take too long. How about seven? That'll give me a couple hours." Georgia nodded back and they both drank their coffee in silence, wondering what their upcoming conversation would bring.

***

Wednesday morning found Jordan and Georgia walking through the woods in silence. It was early, and they'd had their caffeine fix to kick off their day, but the cold was obtrusive, and they couldn't make themselves happy to be outside, even going to one of their favorite places. They were also both a little nervous about what they were going to hear from Victoria.

"Why do you think she never said anything before?" Jordan asked. She saw Georgia jump on her right and huff a breath of air out as she squeezed her hands into fists at her side.

"Geez, you startled me," Georgia said, breathily. "I was in my own head I guess."

"Sorry. I was too, and I can't understand why she never spoke to us before. We've been with her dozens of times."

"I'm not sure," Georgia said, pushing some branches out of their way as they got closer to the clearing. "Maybe she never intended to speak to us, but she wanted to help with the situation with Sawyer? She seemed genuinely concerned about his safety."

"I guess," Jordan conceded, kicking leaves out of the way as she walked.

"And she said she was like us and wouldn't tell anyone, so she can probably be trusted with the secret if she's keeping the same one herself. Plus, she said we have a lot to talk about. That's intriguing." She watched Jordan walking along but not saying anything, her jaw set and lips tight. "Jordan, what's wrong. Isn't it kind of neat to know there's another person out there like us? Why are you so upset?"

Jordan stopped and whipped around to face her friend. "I'm upset because she's known I was like this since I was ten years old! She saw me transform for the first time, she knew I was terrified and struggling with it. She watched for *years* as I worked through it all; learned how to control it, fretted about telling my parents, everything. And I did it all alone when right there was someone who could've eased my mind about things, someone who could've told me I wasn't a freak and I wasn't a weirdo. She could've told me there *was* someone else in this whole, entire world who understood what I was going through. Don't you get it? You had your mom the whole time you were growing up to help you through this. I didn't *have* to feel so alone this whole time, but she let me be that way. I'm having a hard time working out how to be ok with someone who'd make that decision." She started walking again and entered the clearing with Georgia trailing behind her.

"I'm sorry, Jordan," Georgia said softly, struggling to push through the branches Jordan was letting swing back behind her. "I know it had to have been hard on you. I can't imagine what that was like. But why don't you ask her before you get more upset about it? Sawyer was upset you didn't tell him about your abilities before he found out, right? But you had your reasons. Maybe she has her reasons for not revealing herself to you… to *us*… before now."

Jordan closed her eyes, breathed deeply for a few seconds, then opened them again. She tried to soften her look before speaking again quietly. "Thanks for keeping me grounded. "I know you're probably right. It was just really hard and lonely before you came along. I'll try to go into this with as open a mind as possible."

Georgia smiled at her and squeezed her arm. They walked to the log next to the bank of the pond and sat, waiting. After a few minutes, Victoria swam out from behind the willow curtain and stopped before them. They looked at each other for a while before Georgia said, "So, should we change and get this started?"

Victoria ruffled her wings gently and Jordan nodded. They closed their eyes and felt the change settle through them. When it was complete, they opened their eyes again and found themselves much closer to Victoria's level. They both sat and waited for her to begin.

"Hello," she began. "It is nice to see you both again. I am glad you decided to come back to see me so soon."

"You said we had a lot to talk about," Jordan responded flatly.

"That we do," Victoria agreed. "Before I begin with what I desire to tell you, however, I feel I need to offer you my apologies, Miss Jordan. I could not help but overhear your discussion before you arrived in the clearing."

Jordan shifted slightly. "Oh, hey, listen Victoria. That's really not necessary. My emotions have been pretty close to the surface these days with everything going on. I probably just overreacted to you not talking to me, or us, before you did."

"Yeah, we're sure you had your reasons," Georgia agreed.

"It is true I had my reasons," Victoria concurred. "How justifiable they are is likely subject to debate. I do want you to know I did not intend to cause you pain and I did not delight in your loneliness. I know what it is like to be alone. I saw the strength you had within you, and while the things you have gone through were difficult, you have thrived wonderfully. It is admirable." At this she bowed her head in a sign of admiration and respect.

"Thanks," Jordan said, a bit shyly. "So, why *didn't* you reveal yourself, if I may ask?"

"That is difficult to explain satisfactorily without telling you my story, and the story of how I came to be here is long; however, it seems you both already know a part of it."

"What do you mean," Georgia said, bemused. "We only just met you. We don't know anything about your story."

"The story of my coming to be in this place begins with the stories you say your mother told you in the evening time," she said to Georgia. "The story of Edmund Nephiryon and Bernard Onirus is where my story begins as well."

"Wait," Jordan said, stiffening. "That was just a story Georgia's mom made up for her."

"Right," Georgia agreed. "It isn't real. It was just a bedtime story."

"I am afraid you are wrong there," Victoria said quietly. "The story is very real. Their story is, in fact, the origin story of this entire town. The habitants of this town are largely descendants of the families made reference to in your mother's stories. And it appears you, Miss Georgia, are descendant of either the Onirus or Nephiryon family based on your shapeshifting ability since birth. You do not have the visual characteristics or personality traits of the

Nephiryon family, therefore it is likely you possess Onirus blood."

Jordan and Georgia stared at Victoria for a long time without speaking. Finally, Georgia said, "Are you messing with us right now?"

"Yeah, how do we know you didn't just hear the story and are using it to trick us into believing you?" Jordan added.

"I understand your hesitation to believe me. Though, please ask yourselves this; what would I have to gain by deceiving you?" Neither Jordan nor Georgia had an answer for this, so she continued. "I am sharing this information with you because I have overheard your conversations and I strongly believe I may have a theory as to why your townspeople are behaving in an unusual manner. In order to fully explain it, I must make you believe and understand the stories you have been told are true."

Georgia looked to Jordan. "I can't think of any reason why she'd tell us the story was true if it wasn't. Plus, nothing really changes for her if we don't believe her; we could just leave, and she'd continue to exist as she has been. If we *do* hear her out, then maybe we can get some more leads or information about the things going on in town. And you said yourself, wouldn't it be great if it were true? We'd have some answers about what we are."

"You're right, I *did* say it would great if it were true," Jordan said slowly. "And she heard me say that too." She looked back to Victoria. "You said Georgia's probably descendant of Bernard Onirus. That still doesn't explain why I am the way I am and why it started when I was ten. And who are you to know anything about this anyway? We've never seen you in a human form, so you could just be a swan who can talk to other animals. Or maybe you're just someone with abilities like us that likes to tell a good story."

"I can see both your skepticism and stubbornness are strong," Victoria said, her voice a bit tighter. "Please believe me when I say the answers to all of your questions are a part of my story, but I again implore you to understand and accept that the beginning of *all* of our stories is with the tales your mother told you, Georgia. What I can tell you now is that the war between the Nephiryon and Onirus families has never ended. It continues to this day but is masked by everyday events and people. In essence, Edmund is using the strategy in Mr. Poe's Purloined Letter and is hiding his war in plain sight."

"So, if we don't believe you that Georgia's bedtime stories are real, then you won't tell us the rest of the story? What's to stop us from telling you we believe you even if we don't just to hear what else you have to say?" Jordan asked.

"I suppose nothing," Victoria answered quietly. "But you seem like a young woman who does not appreciate her time wasted, and I myself share that trait. I do not believe you will waste my time if you do not want yours wasted as well."

Jordan leaned back a little farther on her haunches and thought about that for a moment. Victoria was right, she didn't like to have her time wasted. And she didn't want to hear what Victoria had to say unless it was potentially true.

"I need time to process what you've told us," she finally responded.

"That is fair," Victoria said, sounding satisfied. "Please do take some time to consider what I have told you. But I implore you not to take too long. Should you choose to hear my story and learn of the things that may be happening in your town, sooner would be preferable for all concerned; or rather, all those concerned with preventing very undesirable things from occurring. Return to me at any time should you choose, and we will continue this conversation. Until then, farewell to you both." She floated away back under the willow curtain and was lost from view.

Jordan and Georgia sat at the edge of the pond for a while before slowly transforming again and beginning their trek back to Jordan's house.

"I don't know what to think," Georgia said as they walked. "I still don't see why she'd lie to us about any of it, but if she's right and there's a war going on around us, why haven't we noticed strange things going on before now?"

"Exactly," Jordan agreed. "Although, maybe something has changed in the war recently and that's caused a ripple effect of other change." Her brow was creased in thought. "If she really doesn't like to have her time wasted though, then her logic is sound for letting us go to think about it. And she's right about The Purloined Letter. Often times, the best place to hide something *is* in plain sight."

"Well, you think about it at work and I'll think about it at home, too. We can discuss it more when I come in later for my shift and we can talk to Sawyer about it when we see him again and see what he thinks. Then we'll make our decision. Deal?"

"Deal." Jordan answered as they arrived in her yard. "I'll talk to you later."

"Is it ok if I come home with you after work and stay here tonight?" Georgia asked, walking toward her car.

"Of course it is! You don't ever have to ask again. This is your house now, remember?" Jordan gave Georgia a quick hug and watched her get in the car and drive away. She sat on the front steps of her house, her chin in her hands and her mind wandering to thoughts of what Victoria might have to say if she was, in fact, telling the truth.

Chapter Sixteen
Auggie's Warning

The day went by in a blur for Jordan. She figured she clearly must have been distracted at work the past couple of days because nothing she normally would have done had been done. The preparation for the week's orders wasn't even started and the store was in disarray when she arrived. Fortunately, these tasks kept her very busy for the better portion of the day. She didn't even notice the tinkle of the bell over the door or the sound of it opening and closing and was, therefore, very surprised when she looked up from her order spreadsheet to see Sawyer standing in front of her. She let out a yelp and gripped the counter tightly.

"Crap, you scared me!" she said, breathing rapidly. She noticed Sawyer looked as handsome as ever, but significantly more tired and slightly disheveled. She thought that was a bit strange since it was only eleven in the morning. Despite his slightly ruffled appearance, she couldn't help focusing on how attractive he was with his tired eyes and messy hair. "Is everything ok?"

Sawyer gave her a small smile and set a cup of coffee down in front of her. "I'm fine; just tired. I planned on coming by to talk to you tomorrow, but I was feeling a little anxious to tell you the stuff I found out. I can tell you the whole story later tonight if you're free. I was able to talk to gramps last night, and some things he told me made me curious. I ended up doing a little bit of extra reconnaissance work on my own to check on some things.

Time sort of got away from me I guess because I haven't actually been to bed yet."

"Oh my gosh!" Jordan exclaimed. "You have to be exhausted. I think maybe you need this more than I do," she said, holding the coffee cup toward him. He put his hand on hers around the cup and pushed it gently back toward her.

"I appreciate the gesture, but I plan on going back home, checking on the animals, grabbing a piece of toast, and taking a nap for a while. Are you free this evening?"

"I am. Georgia's going to come home with me after work, so it actually works out great. Why don't we meet at my house again?"

"That sounds perfect to me. Does Georgia have any more of her mom's cookies? Those were so good."

"I can definitely check with her. Can you be there at six thirty? Will that be enough sleep for you? Georgia and I actually had a little adventure of our own this morning and, depending on what you have to say, we may need to venture into the woods again soon to get some additional information."

"That'll be plenty of sleep. I want to be able to sleep tonight too, so I only plan on taking a couple hour nap just to make myself a little more functional. I'm intrigued by this adventure you had and, I have to be honest, a little nervous at the prospect of going in those woods after dark, but I'll trust your judgement." He leaned over the counter and gave her a quick kiss before turning back to the door. "See you at six thirty. Love you."

"Love you, too," Jordan said. The sound of the bell followed him out and she couldn't help smiling. It felt good to know that, despite everything they had been thought the past few days, he was still able to tell her he loved her so easily. He was the one constant good feeling in all of this. Georgia was wonderful, and she felt very happy to have someone to talk to and share about her condition, but Sawyer's feelings for her transcended anything she ever thought she could have. She would do anything for him, and that was a scary but wonderful feeling.

Jordan looked back down at the order list and forced herself to focus and get back to work. She could easily become distracted again thinking about what Sawyer could have possibly heard from his grandpa that would have warranted him staying up all night but fixating on the unknown would just put her farther behind and she didn't need the added stress if they were going to be dealing with something heavy in their lives. Well, something *else* heavy, she thought, smirking. They had enough of that going on in one way or another. She shook her head and went back to the section she had been reviewing before Sawyer arrived. Georgia would be arriving in an hour for her shift and, if she had enough done, they would be able to discuss the possibilities of Sawyer's news and still get everything finished for Ryan by closing.

***

"Well, I'm impressed," Ryan said, perusing the sections of the store and checking the order list as he went. Jordan and Georgia followed closely behind. He had arrived about twenty minutes before the store was to close and the girls were anxious to leave and meet Sawyer. They were able to come up with a number of possibilities as to what he might want to tell them, but agreed it was just speculation until they could have the real conversation with him, so they had worked hard and gotten all of their paperwork done for the week. "The place looks much better than it did yesterday when I came in. Other than your punch card and a few register transactions, I wasn't sure anyone had been here at all."

"Yeah, it was a rough couple days," Jordan agreed, not even trying to come up with a snide remark to excuse her lack of productivity. "But today was business as usual. We even got the holiday pulls done in the back and the rest of the year should be pretty smooth with that set up, barring any secret releases or unexpected runs on certain titles."

"I also did some dusting of the top shelves this afternoon and got in some of the crevices, so we have a jump on the deep clean you talked about a couple of weeks ago," Georgia added. "The lower shelves might look a little dustier because of the settling, but I plan on attacking those during my next shift, so the place should look tip-top in no time."

Ryan turned to face them, looking surprised but pleased. "That's great, ladies. You've done excellent work. Why don't you both take off a few minutes early? I'll take care of the drawer pulls and close down the store." He had barely finished the last sentence before they had their coats on and were at the door.

"Thanks boss!" Jordan called over her shoulder as she wrenched the door open.

"Yeah, thanks. See you later," Georgia added, shutting the door behind them. They smiled at each other and ran to their cars, anxious to get to Jordan's house and get the next installment of the story they had become so invested in.

They both skidded to a stop on the gravel driveway and barely got their cars turned off before they slammed their doors shut and ran to the front door. It was early, and they knew Sawyer wouldn't arrive for a little while, but they wanted to get snacks and beverages out of the way before they got down to the discussion. Georgia got the coffee brewing while Jordan got some tea out of the refrigerator and set the batch of Amy's cookies Georgia had stopped into her house to grab on their way home. They also put out a package of biscotti and some sliced summer sausage and cheese. This was all laid out on the table along with plates and silverware when Jordan's doorbell rang. They heard the creak of the door opening.

"I saw the cars in the driveway. Are you two in there?" Sawyer called.

"Yes, get in here!" They both yelled back at the same time. They heard him chuckled as his footsteps made their way down the hallway and into the kitchen.

"Wow, check out this spread!" Sawyer said, leaning in and kissing Jordan on the cheek. He reached over and pulled Georgia's long ponytail affectionately before walking to the sink and washing his hands. He grabbed a glass from the cabinet and sat down, poured some iced tea, and popped an entire cookie in his mouth. "If I'd known having a painful conversation with gramps would result in such a feast, I might have been persuaded to do it earlier."

"You're welcome to this kind of spread any time, you know that. My parents love you so I'm not sure I'd even need to be home," Jordan joked as she sat down next to him. "But I do love that you're so comfortable here."

"Judy and Gordon are good at making people feel welcome," Georgia agreed, putting a couple biscotti on her plate and sitting across from Jordan and Sawyer. "I can't believe I'll be moving in here soon. I feel a little silly being grown up and moving in with another family, but at the same time I never had any siblings, so I'm looking forward to the opportunity to have that sister experience even if it's only for a little while."

"Me, too," Jordan said, reaching across the table and giving Georgia's hand a squeeze. "And hopefully it's more than a little while." She turned to Sawyer and took a deep breath. "Ok, so we've been dying to hear what you found out for us."

"Especially since it made you feel the need to pull an all-nighter doing some investigative work," Georgia added.

"I didn't really *have* to do it. I was just intrigued by the information I was given, and I knew once I told you what gramps told me, you'd ask questions I wouldn't be able to answer and that would frustrate you."

"He knows me so well," Jordan laughed, putting her head on his shoulder.

"You're a little predictable when it comes to that," Georgia said, winking. "But let's start with the information you found out before we address your fact gathering."

"Right," Sawyer said, taking a drink. "Well, I know gramps isn't much of a conversationalist, and I figured it'd be like pulling teeth, so I approached the topic at the supper table. I've never seen him leave the table at meal time before clearing his plate, so I figured he'd be a semi-captive audience and I'd have the best chance of getting the most time and information out of him."

"Good thinking," Jordan agreed, and Georgia nodded.

"If you think that was good thinking, you're going to love this," Sawyer smiled. He reached into his pocket and set a small, black tape recorder on the table. "I got the whole conversation on tape. I didn't want to miss or forget anything."

Jordan gasped and snatched the tape recorder, then threw her arms around Sawyer's neck. He and Georgia laughed at her reaction and waited for her to calm down enough to remove the tape recorder from her hand. "Don't crush it, Jordan," Georgia said. "We need to listen to it."

"Right, right, sorry." She released the tape recorder to Georgia who placed it on the table.

"Anway, as soon as I set the bowls of chili down, I told him I wanted to ask him about some things I've noticed around town," Sawyer continued. "He grunted, which isn't a 'no', so I kept going and that's where I started recording." He pushed the play button on the recorder and sat back, taking Jordan's hand.

"So, gramps, my friends and I have noticed a lot of people are acting strange around town. They're not picking up books, food, farm orders, even though they've all been paid for. The number of people overlapping on those lists is hard to ignore. And it's also strange that a lot of people's behavior has changed significantly. Those who were perfectly pleasant and friendly are now acting much more hostile and shady. They aren't seen around town much anymore like they were before, and their activity is all at night, even if they just finished working evening shifts."

There was a long pause on the tape recorder and Sawyer held up his hand to signal them to wait as he saw Jordan's mouth open, presumably to ask what the silence was about.

"Why are you asking me about this? Why not someone else in town?" a familiar, gruff voice finally asked.

"We've found one connecting factor with all the people that seems too significant to be a coincidence. They all either work at the mill or they're related to someone who does," Sawyer answered.

They all heard the quietest intake of breath on the recorder and another shorter pause before Auggie's voice whispered, "You need to be careful there."

Jordan and Georgia had been staring at the recorder, but at these words they turned to Sawyer, eyebrows raised. He gave them a knowing look and remained silent.

"Be careful?" Sawyer's recorded voice asked. "What do you mean? I'm just trying to understand what might be happening in town and if it has anything to do with something that might be going on at the mill. I know it's been a long time since you retired from there, but I hoped you might have some insights."

"The mill's a dark place. People who get out unscathed are lucky. When I worked there, lots of folks just stopped showing up for their shifts. No one ever talked about it or questioned it. One day, Joe Shmoe'd be working next to me on the line. The next day, Joe was gone, and Bob was there; no explanation, no acknowledgement of the change, nothing. Joe wouldn't be seen around town much anymore after that and, if he was, he was busy, distracted, and it'd only be in the evenings. Eventually, everyone would stop paying attention to him and, after a while, he'd disappear for good and never be seen again."

"What do you mean 'disappear'?" Sawyer's voice inquired. "Do you mean disappear like move away, die, what?"

"Don't know for sure," Auggie responded.

Jordan made a frustrated sound and Sawyer put his hand on her thigh as the tape continued.

"Ok," Sawyer continued, and the disappointment in his voice was noticeable to them as well. "So, did anyone ever figure out what caused the changes at the mill; why certain people would get replaced, start acting funny, and then disappear? Do you think what was happening then is happening now, just on a bigger scale maybe?"

"We knew better than to ask questions back then," Auggie answered. "And you should know better now. The mill's a dark place," he repeated. "You should forget what you've noticed, boy." There was a scrape of a chair on a wood floor, and footsteps receding. Sawyer sighed on the tape and it shut off.

Jordan sat back in her chair and Georgia looked down at her cup.

"I'm sorry I couldn't get more out of him," he apologized. "But I was too invested to just stop there. So, that's when I got in my truck and drove to that closed off road behind the mill. I parked deep in the trees and walked around to the side wall on the exterior of the mill; there's one that's crumbling away and has low points. I figured I might be able to climb up part of it and scout a way to get in."

"You went to the mill at night to try to find a way in after your grandpa told you to stay away and forget about everything?" Georgia asked, stunned.

"That's my guy," Jordan said, squeezing his hand. Sawyer smiled and leaned his shoulder into her.

"One of the broken sections of the wall was low enough I was able to get enough of a foothold to climb the rest of the way up. I just sat on top of the wall for a couple of hours, watching shadows move through the lit windows. I figured out one of the areas on the southwest corner was apparently not being used. The lights turned on for a short time every forty-five minutes, a single person would walk back and forth once, then the light would shut off again. My best guess is that it was a security guard checking things out. I decided to go check to see if any of the dark windows on the ground level were unlocked, so I climbed down the other side of the wall and ran through the shadows to the windows. The first few I tried were locked, but one of them was cracked in the corner. I wrapped my flannel shirt around my arm and reached through the broken area to push the lock open. The window opened easy after that. I listened for an alarm and looked for any blinking lights to indicate a silent alarm or motion detectors, but there weren't any. I slid it shut again and waited until the next round of lights came on and someone walked through to make sure no one was coming to check out the window. After they did their routine check, I waited long enough for them to get far away and then opened the window and climbed in."

"You went inside?!" Georgia exclaimed.

Jordan shushed her with a wave of her hand. "What did you see?" she asked eagerly.

"Not much," he answered sadly. "The room was huge. It could have been used for a warehouse, it was so big. Partial walls had been put up, but I could tell they'd been there a long time. Everything was filthy, and the place was almost empty. At one end of the room there was a sectioned off area with a well, and that seemed a little bizarre. I looked down into it and it looked like there was water at the bottom. Maybe it was left over from back in the day before running water or something. There were a few filing cabinets spaced throughout the rest of the room that were locked, and there were four desks like you see in school facing a bigger desk at the front. I don't know for sure, but it looked like it might be where some kind of training took place or something. Anyway, I went to the door the security people came through and it was locked as well. I checked in the garbage can at the front of the room and there was a manila envelope with a couple pieces of paper in it, so I grabbed it and left out the window again. I left it unlocked in case I or we want to go back." He pulled the envelope out of his pocket and set it on the table.

Jordan reached out, took the envelope, and opened it. "They look like employment forms," she said, flipping through them. "There's a personal info form, a bank info form for payroll, and it looks like this is for a mechanic position because there's a safety course confirmation to that effect. Actually, it looks like an almost complete employee file. Wait," she said, flipping back to the first paper. "This is Mr. Neff's file. He's one of the people Mama Landry said was going out late at night and who didn't come in for his book order."

"He never picked up his cheese curds either, remember?" Sawyer added.

"Right! But he's been working at the mill for years," Jordan said, a perplexed look on her file. "Why's his file in a garbage can in a seemingly unused room? Do you think he got fired or something?"

"Mama Landry said she's seen him going out at night after working his shifts at the mill," Georgia reminded her. "He would've been fired pretty recently if that's the case."

"That's true," Jordan said absentmindedly, clearly deep in thought. "If he didn't get fired though, why would they throw away his file?"

"Maybe he's working a different position so they threw away his mechanic file?" Sawyer offered.

"Wouldn't they just get rid of the mechanic part of it and keep the rest of the stuff that still applies though?" Georgia asked.

They all sat in silence, thinking about the situation for a while.

"I think we need to talk to Victoria," Jordan finally said.

Georgia and Sawyer looked at her. Georgia's look was one of uncertainty and Sawyer's was one of confusion.

"But she told us not to come back unless we believed what she told us about mom's stories being true. The last we discussed things, you weren't quite a believer yet."

"I'm sorry, who's Victoria?" Sawyer asked, raising his hand.

"She's the swan from the pond in the clearing," Jordan said by way of answer to Sawyer's question. She turned to Georgia. "I've been thinking about it. I don't know that I completely believe it, but I also don't completely disbelieve it. I want to go back and tell her I accept that her story *could* be true, and I'll be more likely to believe it if the rest of what she has to say falls in line with the things we're experiencing now in town. I think she might be receptive to that."

"Ok, so I can tell you think you answered my question," Sawyer said in forced patience, "but you really haven't. A swan in a pond doesn't tell me anything. When did you talk to her? *How* did you talk to her? And why is anything she has to say important?"

"We only just spoke to her for the very first time the night you saw us change. She told us to follow you and try to ease your mind. Before we left, she told us to come and see her again because we had a lot to talk about." Georgia explained.

"Yeah, she's the whole adventure thing I told you about at the store," Jordan said, picking up the story. "When we went back later to talk to her, she told us this bedtime story Georgia's mom used to tell her was actually true. It's about these two feuding magical families from a long time ago that started a war. She said it's still going now, but it's masked by everyday events and people. She wouldn't tell us the rest of the story unless we were willing to believe what she said was true, so I told her I needed time to think about what I believed. I was waiting to hear from you and what you found out from Auggie before I decided whether I wanted to go back to talk to her."

"Why weren't you willing to believe what she told you?" Sawyer asked.

"Because it sounds ridiculous!" Jordan said incredulously. "Wouldn't you think it sounded insane if someone told you that a bunch of magic families used to exist, and the two biggest, most powerful ones started a war, stripped everyone else of their power, and that war was still going on today but somehow no one knows about it?!"

Sawyer took Jordan's face gently in both of his and looked into her eyes. "Jordan, if anyone had ever told me that there were people in this world that could turn into animals, I would have had them committed." Jordan swallowed hard and cast her eyes down toward the floor. "I'm starting to understand there are probably a lot of things in this world I'm not going to believe or understand right away, but that doesn't mean they aren't true or real or that I shouldn't at least listen to an attempt at an explanation. I'm sure glad I listened to yours."

Jordan looked at him for a minute and then leaned forward to kiss him lightly.

"He's right, Jordan," Georgia said quietly. "I think we may need to accept the fact that our abilities might just be a very small part of something much bigger that's going on around here and Victoria could know more about what's behind it all."

Jordan sighed deeply. "Ok. You're both probably right. We can all go talk to her tomorrow."

"Actually, I think you two should go," Sawyer said. "I won't be able to hear anything she has to say anyway, and I think I'm going to go fill out an application at the mill office tomorrow."

"What?!" Jordan and Georgia exclaimed at the same time.

"Come on," Sawyer said in a placatory tone. "All of the weirdness going on seems to stem from there and now there's this thing with Mr. Neff's file. I think we're going to need a mole in there eventually. I might as well get the ball rolling with this. You go and talk to swan lady tomorrow and I'll stop by the mill after work at the grocery café. We can meet up after we're all done. You can fill me in on what she has to say, and I can let you know how things went with the application. We can work on what else I can do to help after that." He smiled softly at their looks of concern. "I'll be careful. I'm really good at blending in and flying under the radar. We have to get to the bottom of what's going on around here. This is how I can help."

"Please promise me you'll be beyond careful," Jordan said in a worried tone. "No information you could gather would be worth me losing you."

Sawyer pulled her in to his chest and hugged her tight. "You aren't going to lose me. And I'm not doing anything other than information gathering. Nothing's going to happen. I'll talk to people I feel can be trusted, I'll observe what I see going on, and I'll bring the info back to you guys. Once we have what we need, I'll quit. No harm, no foul." Georgia's face was worried too, and Sawyer reached out, took her hand, and squeezed it gently. She forced a smile onto her face and squeezed his hand back. He smiled and put his arm back around Jordan. "You two are great to be so worried about me. I promise to be careful."

Jordan pulled away and rubbed her hands on her jeans. "Ok, so Georgia and I'll go talk to Victoria tomorrow afternoon. Sawyer, you put in your application tomorrow after work. Sawyer can come by tomorrow evening after he gets back from the mill and we can trade info. Georgia, I'll fill you in on what Sawyer tells me when we work together the next day. Is everyone in agreement?"

They all nodded. Sawyer got up, kissed Jordan on top of the head, and grabbed a couple more cookies. "Good luck you guys," he said, knuckle bumping Georgia's shoulder as he headed out the kitchen toward the front door. "You both be careful too," they heard him call from the front hall. "There are crazy things out there in those woods." They could hear the smile in his voice and couldn't help but smile themselves as the door closed behind him. They heard the engine of his truck catch and the sound of him driving away.

"I have an uneasy feeling in my stomach," Jordan said. "I don't like the idea that he went to that mill once, much less him working in it."

"I don't either, but hopefully he won't have to for long. Once we hear what Victoria has to say, maybe we can solve whatever the issue is, and he can stop sooner rather than later."

"I hope so." Jordan agreed.

Chapter Seventeen
Victoria's Story

"Victoria!" Jordan howled. She and Georgia had been sitting at the end of the pond for nearly ten minutes in their animal forms waiting for Victoria to arrive. "She usually comes out right after we get here," Jordan said to Georgia. "Where is she?"

"I don't know," Georgia answered, laying down. "Maybe she isn't here."

"I've never seen her anywhere else. Oh wait, I think I see her." Sure enough, they could just spot Victoria through the willow branches. It was another few minutes before she slowly floated through them and made her way to the edge of the pond where they were waiting.

"My apologies," Victoria said softly. "I was finishing up a task. I hope you have not waited long."

"Only a few minutes," Georgia rose and answered quickly before Jordan could say anything. "Is everything ok with you?"

"A friend is upset with me, but we have been through much worse. It will pass. I assume you have returned because you have decided whether you can believe my story."

"We have," Jordan said. "I feel like I should be honest and tell you it's hard for me to believe what you said, but I can't deny it's as good an explanation as any. I'm willing to accept that it's quite possibly true and I'm very interested to hear if the rest of the story falls in line with the things happening in our town."

"I respect your honesty. I understand it must be hard to accept what I say as fact and I appreciate your open mind. If you please, I would like to share the rest of my story with you, but I must warn you that it iss even more phantasmagorical than what you have had to accept thus far. At times, even I find it hard to believe it has happened, yet this is the reality I am faced with."

"I know that feeling," Jordan admitted. "We promise to listen and be receptive to everything you tell us."

Victoria ruffled her feathers and continued. "The story is long. Please be comfortable." Jordan and Georgia both lowered themselves onto the frost-covered grass, their tails wrapped close to them for warmth, and looked at Victoria expectantly.

"It has been over two thousand years now since the events involving me directly unfolded, and since the events of Edmund and Bernard's battle. Your mother told you Bernard defeated Edmund and stopped the use of magic immediately after so as to prevent any such war from arising again. Unfortunately, that is not where the story ends." She paused as if steeling herself. "Edmund lives. A maid in the household watched through a cracked door and witnessed what were thought to be his final moments and recounted what she saw to her husband later. Edmund reached for his amulet just as life was leaving his human form and managed to transform to his animal state; a large raven. He still exists in this form, but he is weakened. He is said to have retreated to a hideaway and continues to plan his return to power."

"Two *thousand* years later and he's still alive?!" Jordan asked, raising her head quickly.

"Yes. The magic in our blood keeps us alive much longer than non-magical humans. Edmund's sorcerers and alchemists were very powerful, and we believe they may have managed to find ways to keep him alive even beyond a normal magical life span. Immortality has even been considered. It is said his current dwelling is hidden somewhere on his old land and he communicates with secret followers in their animal forms. He provides them instructions and directions to recruit followers into his army and continue his ambitions to control this land; possibly more."

"And you know this how?" Georgia asked, in a very respectful, inquisitive tone.

"Well, to answer that, I must give you a little of my background."

"Please do," Jordan said.

"You see, I am also descendent of Bernard Onirus, but I fell in love with a man who was Edmund's most trusted alchemist as well as his great, great nephew. The details of that story can be saved for another time, but this man by the name of Christian was closer to Edmund than anyone at that time and knew his innermost secrets. He stayed with him through his loss in battle and was privy to his existence and relocation. All of this he eventually divulged to me."

"Why would he do that?" Jordan asked, trying to keep the skepticism out of her voice.

"And how did you even come in contact with him if you were from feuding families?" Georgia added.

"Christian's father and grandfather had both been alchemists for Edmund before him and had served him loyally. Christian, however, did not agree with Edmund's ultimate goal of solitary control over the land and the people. He did not desire to follow in their footsteps. He met me in these very woods during one of the many walks he took to clear his mind and think of ways he could possibly abdicate his role without being killed for acts of treason. He learned of my lineage when he saw me changing from my swan form back to my human form. We met here often after that, and we grew to love each other deeply. We agreed to abandon our familial duties and run away together, but Christian could not bring himself to do this until he accomplished two goals. The first was to stop Edmund from being able to recruit more soldiers. The second was to be sure we would both be safe and unable to be found once we escaped. He finally came up with a solution to solve both issues at once, but it was a dangerous endeavor. He planned to steal the amulet from Edmund."

"Steal the amulet from the most powerful guy around? A man who thought this guy was his right-hand man; his most trusted follower?" Jordan asked. She couldn't help being intrigued, despite herself.

"Correct," Victoria answered. "Christian knew Edmund's schedule well and came up with a sleeping draught to give him additional time in which to complete his task. He gave the draught to Edmund and everyone in his court by putting it in their drinks with supper. As soon as it took effect, Christian removed the amulet and ran. We had previously made plans to meet at the edge of the woods half way between Edmund's compound and my home. However, Christian was unaware of the additional troops outside the compound due to a wave of recruitment that had taken place that evening. He thought he managed to elude them, but he was followed. He attempted to evade his pursuers by taking a complicated, twisted path to our meeting place, but the delay made me concerned something had happened to him. I had just started to make my way out of the woods toward Edmund's compound when I saw him running toward me, followed by four of Edmund's men. Christian called for me to run and hide, but I was not swift enough. He caught up to me, followed closely by the others. We ran through the woods to our clearing in the hopes of being able to hide behind the willows, but one of the men's arrows struck me."

"No," Georgia whispered. Victoria nodded.

"I fell at the edge of the pond and lay there, dying. Christian was shot as well, but it was a superficial wound. As he fell, he changed into his animal form and was able to fight off the men by overpowering them. The darkness had apparently hidden from them the fact that the bear was, in fact, Christian. Only one of Edmund's men made it out of the woods alive. We found out later that man told Edmund their shot at Christian had been lethal, but then the beast came along, killing the other three men and forcing him to retreat before he could obtain the amulet or Christian's body. The man was killed for his failures and Edmund was no longer able to recruit followers without his amulet."

"But what about you!?" Jordan cried. "You were dying."

"I was. And I did, in a way. Christian made his way back to my weakening body and returned to his human form. He was able to work enough magic to concoct a potion. He then poured the potion into the pond to combine with the water. He placed my dying body into the water. As life slowly left my human form, I was changed to this form where I have remained to this day. I must remain in this pond for the potion to keep me alive. Finally, he transformed the amulet to look like an ordinary rock and tossed it into the bottom of our pond to be hidden here forever."

They all sat in silence for what seemed like ages; the girls processing what they just heard, and Victoria patiently waiting for the questions she knew would follow.

"I'm so sorry," Jordan finally whispered in a huff of breath. Victoria's delicate head turned to her in surprise. "Your story is so tragic and I… I accused you of being selfish for not showing yourself to me and helping me. I was the selfish one."

"You did not know," Victoria said graciously. "I harbor no resentment toward you whatsoever for your understandable anger and frustration. I wanted many times to speak to you, Jordan, but Christian and I decided it would be safer for all of us to refrain." Jordan nodded her head in understanding.

"Victoria," Georgia interjected quietly. "Everyone you've mentioned so far has magical lineage. You said I'm likely descendent of it as well. What does your story have to do with Jordan and her magic?"

"Ah, yes. Fairly recently in the grand scheme of things, Jordan's story intersects mine," Victoria said. Her tone was hard to read. They couldn't tell if she sounded wistful or possibly contrite. "Jordan, do you remember back to the day of your first transformation; what was it you did shortly before the bear came along?"

"Um," Jordan said, trying to recall the specific details of the day. "I know it was hot and I was sitting on the bank of the pond."

"It *was* hot," Victoria agreed. "And what did you do to rectify that situation?"

"I put my feet..." Jordan trailed off, looking from Victoria to Georgia and then down at the pond. "... in the water... to cool off."

"Correct," Victoria nodded. "And do you remember anything about how you felt when you did that?"

It came back to Jordan in a rush. "It felt cool, but not just on my feet!" she said excitedly, rising off the grass and pacing back and forth. "I remember thinking it was odd the cooling sensation was all the way in my chest and stomach. And suddenly I could hear things better and see things better; like all my senses had sharpened!"

"Yes," Victoria said sadly. "You were affected by the magic in the water. Just as Edmund had been using the amulet to recruit soldiers, the amulet's power seems to have leached into the already potion-affected water, so you touched the water which had the same effect on you. You were able to change from that point on."

"It makes so much sense!" Jordan howled, relief washing over her. She finally had the answer to what had happened to her to cause her abilities. The relief slowly faded as additional questions flooded into her mind. "But, wait. If it's Edmund's amulet that caused me to change, doesn't that mean I have some of the magic of his blood in me somehow? I mean, doesn't that make me…"

"It does not," Victoria answered firmly before Jordan could finish. "Magic is pure. It is not good or evil; it just is. The good and evil in this world lies within people and the way they choose to use that magic, as well as the intent in their actions and decisions. Christian used magic he had learned and used in service of Edmund to keep me alive out of love. You, Jordan, have made your difficult decisions largely to protect others. You sacrificed having friends and love until recently to protect them and yourself from the truth and the negative ramifications that could result from that knowledge. That kind of selflessness cannot come from a place of evil."

Jordan took that in for a bit and sat back on her haunches again. "I suppose," she conceded. Georgia rose and walked over to sit next to Jordan. She leaned gently against her. Jordan leaned against her as well, grateful for the comfort. It was a lot to take in at once.

"Victoria, I do have another question." Georgia said.

"Please, ask it. I will answer anything I can."

"Well, your story explains why you're here and how Jordan became the way she is. What I don't understand is, if the amulet's hidden here in the pond and Edmund's no longer able to recruit troops, how is the war able to continue? What does this have to do with what's happening now?"

A soft sigh escaped Victoria's delicate body and it was another while before she answered. "I will always be grateful for what Christian did for me, and I know he did it out of love, but his act of love for me came at a steep price. Edmund *was*, in fact, unable to recruit for many years without his amulet. It seemed the war was to come to an end. Then, a few decades ago, Christian was on one of his nighttime visits to the edge of Edmund's property and noticed there seemed to be more activity than usual. He chanced going closer to the main house and, while he did not see Edmund, he was able to hear what was, unmistakably, an initiation ceremony. He knew them well as he had been a part of them when he was serving Edmund himself. He did not know how at the time, but Edmund was taking on members of his army again. After many months, Christian found his way secretly into the mill and was able to deduce they have a well at the mill whose water has magical elements; the same magical elements, it seems, as this pond."

"Oh, no!" Jordan and Georgia exclaimed.

"Oh, yes," Victoria said sadly. "It seems this pond is connected through a deep underground spring to the well at the mill. While the pond is keeping me alive, it is also giving Edmund the ability to continue recruiting for his war. I have begged Christian to drain the water from this pond, but he refuses."

"Of course he does!" Jordan barked, shocked she would suggest such a thing. "He loves you! He risked everything for you. You're probably the one good thing he has going in this world. He doesn't want to lose you."

"And I love him deeply for it," Victoria agreed. "But is one life, even the life of someone we love deeply, worth the loss of many others? I cannot agree with that. He has spent all his efforts these past many years trying to develop potions to bring me back to my human form as well as to make himself wholly animal. He has succeeded in creating a potion to make him an animal permanently, but as his animal form is not the same as mine, it would not make sense to use it. He is far more valuable to humanity in his human form, and we are still able to communicate and be together in this way. I have told him he should sacrifice me to save potentially hundreds of others, but he will not hear it. And I cannot make him." Her voice cracked here, and she was quiet for a minute. Her voice was stronger when she continued. "So, here we are. It appears from what you have told me and from what my Christian has witnessed in his nighttime ventures that Edmund has increased his recruiting numbers by a substantial percentage. The mill has been hiring more people than usual and many of the existing workers are apparently being affected. They have started hiring on the spot and training the same day in some cases. We fear he may be bolstering his numbers in preparation for an imminent, large attack of some kind."

"Oh, God," Jordan said, terror in her voice. "Sawyer!" Georgia gasped as she caught up to what Jordan was thinking.

"What does this information have to do with your gentleman friend?" Victoria asked, confusion in her voice.

"Sawyer's been helping us do some investigative work to try to determine what's going on with the people in town," Jordan explained. "He asked his grandpa, Augustus Toole, about the mill since he retired from there many years ago. Auggie told him the mill was a dark place and people who made it out unscathed were lucky."

"He is not wrong," Victoria agreed. "But I still do not understand your alarm."

"Well, what Auggie told him made Sawyer curious, so he went to the mill last night to see if he could figure out any more information. He broke into a window on the back side where he said it looked like there wasn't much activity." Victoria flapped her wings in alarm at this, but Jordan pressed on. "He was only able to get into one room and no one was there, but he found a folder with a man's file in it and he brought it to us after he left the mill. The file belonged to one of the men who's been acting strange and who's been going out late at night after he was supposed to have worked all afternoon and evening."

"Oh, and he said he saw a well in that room!" Georgia shouted. "I wonder if it's the same one that's connected to this pond!"

"It likely is," Victoria said, gravely. "But why were you so upset when you said his name before? Based on what you have told me, your friend made it out safely. With the information I have provided, you can tell him it would not be wise to go back there again."

"That's just it," Jordan said, desperation in her voice. "He *is* going there this afternoon to apply for a job. He wanted to get insider information and work as a mole until we got all the information we needed from the place!"

"Oh, dear," Victoria gasped, fear in her voice as well. "You must stop him. A young man of his strength and intelligence would be a great addition for Edmund. Leave now, please! Go find your friend and stop him before the damage is irreparable! Come back to me when you have him, and we will work together to determine a way to keep us all as safe as possible."

Jordan and Georgia spun around and tore off toward Jordan's house, both hoping they could catch Sawyer before it was too late.

Chapter Eighteen
Rescue Attempt

Jordan and Georgia changed back to their human forms at the edge of the woods and continued running to Jordan's car. Georgia barely had the passenger door shut before Jordan spun out of the driveway, spraying gravel behind her.

"Where are you going to try to find him first?" Georgia said, hanging on to the dash to steady herself as Jordan took corners twenty miles per hour over the speed limit.

"We should try the farm. He would've wanted to shower and change before he went to apply for a job, even one at a mill. If we miss him, it probably won't be by much and, though I don't want it to come to this, we could check with Auggie to make sure he wasn't going somewhere else before the mill."

Georgia shuddered as Jordan rounded another corner, the tires of her car screeching slightly. "I'll let you have that conversation," she said.

"I'd be willing to deal with the devil himself if it meant stopping Sawyer from going in that mill."

"You're right," Georgia agreed as they turned onto the dirt lane that lead to the farm house where Sawyer and his grandpa lived. "I would too, of course."

Jordan jumped out of the car without even turning off the engine. Her headlights shined on the wood front door as she ran to it with Georgia right behind her. She banged loudly on the door and waited.

"Jordan, look," Georgia pointed next to the barn where Sawyer's truck was parked.

"Oh, thank god," Jordan exhaled as the door opened and Augustus Toole stood in front of them, blocking the dim light from within with his hulking figure. Even at ninety something years old, he was still a formidable man and Jordan and Georgia both took a small step back.

"What the hell are you kids doing; trying to break down the damn door?!" Augustus barked at them.

Jordan tried to speak, but her voice wouldn't come. She cleared her throat and tried again. "We're sorry to bother you Mr. Toole," Jordan said, and was relieved to hear her voice project at a relatively confident sounding volume. "We were hoping to catch Sawyer before he left to put in his job application. Can we please speak to him?"

"He's not here," Augustus said gruffly. "He asked to borrow my truck for the interview because he thought it would make a better impression. I don't know why anyone would care what kind of car he'd drive for an interview, but the boy does a lot to help me around here and I didn't need it tonight, so I let him have it." He peered at Jordan and Georgia as the relief they had felt at the sight of Sawyer's truck drained away and their faces registered the terror that was resettling. "Where's he applying anyway?"

"He's going to the mill, Mr. Toole," Jordan said, a small catch in her voice. She noticed the corners of the man's mouth tighten at these words. "Please, sir, do you know if he was going to stop anywhere else before going there?"

"I don't, missy. But I hope he does, and you can catch him before he gets there." His gnarled old hand grabbed the edge of the door and as he closed it slowly he muttered, "Otherwise none of us may ever see him again."

Jordan thrust her foot between the door and the jamb, preventing the door from shutting all the way. She leaned her face into the small crack left open and asked loudly, "What do you mean by that, Mr. Toole? Do you know more about what's going on there than you told him the other night? Is he in danger? Why would we never see him again?" There was no answer and Jordan drew a shallow, shaky breath before she forced the next words. "Please, Mr. Toole. I love your grandson. I need to try to help him, but to do that, I need *you* to help *us*."

The door slowly reopened, and the old man's face was stony as he looked at the two girls. "If he's inside that mill, there's nothing you can do but wait and hope for the best. There's no way in or out other than the front door."

"Sawyer found a low point in the wall behind the mill and was able to get into a room the other night," Georgia piped up from behind Jordan. "He said there were desks, some filling cabinets, and a well in the room. But he couldn't get anywhere else."

Augustus shifted his gaze to her, his eyebrows raised. "Did he, now?" He rubbed his stubbled, grey chin in thought. "They must be getting sloppy on their security. That room is the training room, or it was almost forty years ago. Once someone was hired, they had three days of training in that room. The people who were suddenly replaced were taken to that room too for their transfer meetings. They said it was to fill out more paperwork for reassignment, but I don't believe it."

"Why not?" Georgia asked intently.

"Because we never saw them in the mill again after that. If they'd been reassigned in the mill, someone would've seen them in there. They may have been reassigned, but it was to somewhere other than the mill. Even if they'd been sent to the ravine town to work, they should've still been seen or heard from, but no one ever was. After a while they just…"

"Disappeared," Jordan finished in a whisper at the same time Augustus finished his sentence.

"Sawyer's a good boy," Augustus said. "He's done a lot to help me around here and he has this place running better than it ever has. The boy has a knack for running a farm." He noticed Jordan's anguished face and reached out to pat Jordan's shoulder. "He's a smart boy, too. They'll surely want to take him on, but he may be smart enough to avoid whatever evil is going on inside those walls. I did." Jordan looked at Augustus with tears in her eyes. "You two get going and try to catch him before he goes in there. But if you don't, you make sure you stay out of there. You go on home and wait for him. I'll send him 'round when he gets back here, I promise you that. Between his smarts and your determination, you might be able to save him yet."

Jordan could only nod as Georgia grabbed her arm and pulled her toward the car. "Thank you, Mr. Toole," Georgia called over her shoulder. "We'll do that." She opened the passenger door and helped Jordan in before running around and getting in the driver's seat. She turned the car around and accelerated back down the drive. She could see the door to the farm house in the rearview mirror and watched as Mr. Toole slowly shut it behind them. "Jordan, come on. You need to snap out of it. We have to do everything we can to try to save him. Mr. Toole said he'd help and send Sawyer over if he came home."

"If," Jordan said softly.

"When," Georgia said insistently. "He's going to be ok, Jordan. Mr. Toole was right; Sawyer's a smart guy. He knows something's going on. He's got an edge going in, if he's even in at all. He knows better than to be sucked into whatever's happening there. Hopefully we can stop him before he has to use those smarts, but on the off chance he gets in, he might come back with some important information *and* he won't ever have to go back. We'll tell him what Victoria told us and she said we would work out how to keep us all safe."

Jordan took a deep breath and squared her shoulders. "Ok," she said, lacking some of the usual determination in her voice, but sounding better than before. "You're right. We need to stay positive and focused. He'd do the same for us, right?"

"Absolutely," Georgia agreed, painted a forced smile on her face, and steered the car out of town into the darkness of the woods toward the hulking metal gate to the mill's parking lot entrance.

As soon as they arrived and pulled the car to a stop, they realized they'd forgotten one detail; they had no idea what Mr. Toole's vehicle looked like. They knew it was a truck, but that only narrowed down their number of choices in the parking from twenty to seventeen. They walked between the rows of trucks, trying to look as inconspicuous as possible while peering into the windows looking for clues as to which one might belong to Auggie or had recently been used by Sawyer. After two passes, Jordan waved to Georgia to get her attention and, when she came over, pointed through the passenger window of a newer looking black truck. Georgia looked in and, seeing nothing, shrugged her shoulders at Jordan who gestured again emphatically. Georgia looked a second time and saw on the floor there was a flannel jacket. It was the same jacket Sawyer had worn a dozen times before when they hung out. There was no guarantee it was his, but the likelihood was high.

Despondent, they both walked slowly back to Jordan's car and sat in silence for a bit. Suddenly, Jordan sat up straight and looked at Georgia. "Mr. Toole was right. Sawyer's a great, smart guy. They won't be able to corrupt him. He just has to get through his application and possible interview situation and he'll be out of there."

"Absolutely," Georgia agreed, drawing on Jordan's renewed optimism. "If we leave now, he'll probably be back shortly after us with all kinds of information we can share with Victoria."

"You're right," Jordan said, starting the car and pulling out of the parking lot. "I think we should head back to my house, leave a note for him on the door to meet us in the clearing, and be there when he arrives so we can get a jump on things." Georgia nodded, and they rode the rest of the way back to Jordan's house in silence, pondering what events might be taking place in the mill at that very moment and hoping all the terrible things that kept popping into their minds were just products of their imaginations running wild.

***

"I wish there was something I could do to ease your minds," Victoria said as Jordan and Georgia paced back and forth across the bank of the pond. They had changed to their animal forms immediately upon arriving and shared with Victoria the events of the evening; the conversation with Mr. Toole and their observations in the mill parking lot. They then lapsed into silence, pacing anxiously, and had continued to do so for the better part of an hour.

"I just wish we knew something, *anything*, that was going on in there," Jordan said, frustration clear in her voice. "Not knowing is driving me crazy. I'm so worried."

"Your worry is understandable, but I hope it is not warranted," Victoria said, consolingly. "Perhaps I could see if Christian might be willing to…" she trailed off as a soft, low rumble emanated from behind the willow curtain. "Then again, perhaps not," she amended, a slight touch of exasperation in her voice.

"Do you think he'd be able to see what's going on at the mill?" Georgia pressed in an attempt to confirm what Victoria had been about to say. "Surely someone as good and righteous as the person you've described would be willing to help us see if our friend is safe."

"I had hoped he would," Victoria said, sadly. "But he is rarely willing to stray too far from. He almost lost me once and is far less willing to risk it again. In fact, he has tried for the past may decades to prevent anyone from coming to this place any longer. He has been largely successful, but not completely, and this gives him angst. He only deals with it because it means so much to me that he leaves visitors alone." She paused here, her delicate head tilted slightly in contemplation. "Or perhaps I should say he leaves them relatively safe."

"Who else has come here that he's tried to keep away?" Jordan asked.

"Who else? Why, no one else but you and your friend two friends," Victoria answered, a bit of amusement in her voice.

"What?! You mean Christian tried to keep Georgia and me away from here? When? We've never seen anyone else anywhere near here, and definitely no one has ever tried to make us leave."

"You have seen no person here, that is true," Victoria agreed. "But he has been here all the same and has made multiple attempts to persuade you to leave."

Jordan opened her mouth to argue the fact, but the sound of crashing in the distant forest drew all their attentions to the direction of the noise.

"What in the world?" Georgia asked, tilting her head to better hear and determine the source of the noise. They all listened, and it was a few seconds before they could just barely make out the sound of a voice yelling, but they couldn't make out the words. "Is there seriously someone out here running around this late in this cold? Why would anyone…"

"Oh, no," Jordan whispered, almost inaudibly. "I know that voice. And I know who would be out here at this time of night in this cold." She seemed frozen to the spot, her eyes peering through the woods, looking toward the sound. As they waited there, the voice grew louder and more distinguishable, and the cries of "help" and "get away from me" made Jordan's blood run cold.

"We have to help him," Georgia cried, nudging Jordan to move. Just as they took their first steps in preparation to run, they saw a distant form appear deep in the bushes. Shortly after, two additional forms in dark clothing appeared behind the first form. Both dark clothed forms were carrying something shiny in their hands.

"Run," Jordan screamed, though it came out as a high-pitched howl to the humans preparing to enter the clearing.

Jordan ran full speed, not toward Sawyer, who was a few strides in front of her, but toward the men behind him. Her intent was primal; she needed to destroy the threat to the man she loved. She wanted to sink her teeth into their throats until there was no longer breath in their body and her love was safe from these evil creatures. She passed Sawyer, who looked at her in fear and held up his hands as if trying to stop her, but she would not be deterred. She was only a few feet away from them when two loud shots rang out, sounding to her heightened hearing like two small explosions. The first shot whizzed ahead of her into the clearing and the second brushed through the fur on her right shoulder as she collided with the man closest to her, knocking him to the ground and sending them both rolling. Jordan regained her footing first and turned, leaping on the man lying prone on the ground. The man let out a scream as her teeth found the back of his neck and her claws tore through the coat he was wearing and found the soft skin of his back and side. She let go of his neck and pawed at him hard, rolling him to his side. She leaped to the other side of him, so they were eye to eye and she thrilled at the sight of panic in his eyes. He reached around for the gun that had fallen from his hands as he hit the ground, but Jordan knew he would never reach it in time.

Knowing she needed to speak with this man, she closed her eyes and willed herself to calm down enough to transform back to her human form. Upon the completion of her change, she immediately lunged for the gun and turned it on the man, who had stopped struggling to reach it and held his hands up in front of him, still as a stone and shock on his face.

"Why are you chasing him," she asked quietly, still breathing hard. He didn't answer, and she aimed the gun directly at his forehead. "Tell me why you were chasing him, or I'll kill you now."

It was a few seconds before the man found his voice, which shook as he said softly, "I didn't know there were any of you left."

Jordan was taken aback by this, temporarily forgetting her original question. "Any of me?"

"Descendants of Onirus. We were told there were no more active descendants of Bernard Onirus and that our war was only against the ignorant fools with no magic in their blood. Master will be interested to know you still exist."

"Oh, I doubt your *master* will ever get the chance to find out. Especially if you don't tell me why you were chasing Sawyer. Now!" she shouted, and the man jumped.

"He applied to the mill this evening and we knew our master would be very interested in recruiting him to our ranks. When we brought him back to the training room and explained his new role, he was hesitant." The man smirked malevolently. "They always are at first. But we offered generous compensation and, when that did not work, we assured him that, should he not join us, we would punish him and the ones he loves. He disabled the recruiting soldier and was able to escape through an unlocked window in the training room and scaled a low section of the wall outside. We couldn't have anyone sharing our objectives within the mill, so we were instructed to find him and… neutralize the situation. We followed his vehicle from the parking lot to a lot at the other end of town. He left his car and ran on foot into the woods; to this place." The man stopped here and winced as he shifted his weight and blood dripped from his bleeding neck.

"You need to leave," Jordan said, backing slowly away from the man. "Leave this place and don't ever come back here. Leave Sawyer, his grandfather, and all of us alone. You can tell your master, *Edmund*, that you killed Sawyer; he won't bother you again."

The man smiled nefariously, despite the amount of pain was in. "You aren't in a position to make negotiations, girly," he hissed.

"No, it is you who is not in that position!" came a deep, male voice woven into a roar from behind Jordan. She turned around and gasped, stumbling backward away from the man on the ground. An enormous bear had appeared from behind the willow curtain, teeth gleaming and enormous in the small amount of moonlight shining through the dense trees. He charged toward Jordan and the man, stopping to raise up on his hind legs, towering close to seven feet over them. The bear fell forward onto the man and his screams echoed into the night. Jordan fell backward and scurried backwards in a crab walk, the gun still clutched in her hand. She stopped and began to raise the gun before something in her brain made her stop. She had heard the bear yell at the man; heard words through the roar. How could that be unless... he was another shapeshifter. And as he was tearing the man apart, she had to hope he was another shapeshifter who was on their side. She tore her eyes away from the horror happening in front of her and scrambled to her feet, taking off back toward the pond where a different scene of horror was waiting for her.

Georgia had transformed back into her human form as well and was kneeling next to a still figure on the ground. Jordan ran to her and gasped, falling to her knees on the other side of the figure she now recognized as Sawyer. He was lying supine on the grass which had been stained red with the blood flowing from a wound in his back.

Chapter Nineteen
Sacrifice

"Sawyer," Jordan choked, laying the back of her shaking hand on his cheek. His eyes flickered opened and moved in her direction, though she wasn't sure he could see her. "Sawyer, please…"

"Did you stop them?" he whispered. Jordan looked to Georgia who nodded, indicating the other man was no longer a threat.

"Yes. Yes, we got them. They won't be able to hurt anyone again." Jordan answered.

"Good," Sawyer nodded, his breath came out in a soft gurgle and a small drop of blood appeared at the corner of his mouth. Jordan reached down and wiped it away. "There are more," he continued. "Need… to stop them."

"Shhh," Jordan said, brushing the hair off his clammy forehead. "You've done enough. You did so well," Jordan sobbed and paused, trying to steady her voice. "All you need to worry about now is resting. You have to get your strength back." She looked at Georgia, tears flowing down her face. She could see Georgia had been crying as well, and her resolve strengthened a bit. "We need to get him to a doctor," she whispered, urgently.

"He will not make it," the deep voice said from behind them. They turned and saw a tall, slim, dark-haired man; his face, shirt, and hands were stained dark crimson and were wet with blood. "He has lost too much blood. I anticipate he has but minutes." He walked toward them slowly and they tensed but didn't leave Sawyer's side.

"No," Jordan said, not as a declaration but a desperate plea. She looked up at him and something in her mind registered. "You're Christian, aren't you?"

Georgia looked back and forth between the man and Jordan, then suddenly seemed to make the connection too. With a gasp, she said "You're the one, the bear who's tried to keep us away from this place! You tried to chase me out of the woods that day when Jordan and I first saw each other change!"

"And he saw me change the first time it ever happened," Jordan said softly. The man nodded in assent. Jordan looked back down at Sawyer. She could see his skin was growing paler, even in the darkness of the woods. "Please, Christian, isn't there anything you can do? I can't lose him," her voice caught, and she was unable to continue.

"I am sorry," Christian said softly.

Jordan believed him. From his look of absolute despair to the tone of sadness in his voice, it was clear to her his words were true. After all, this had to be bringing back some truly awful memories for him and her heart ached a bit extra for him, but she couldn't focus on anyone but Sawyer at the moment. Her gaze shifted to the pond where Victoria floated in beautiful silence and a single, silver tear dropped from her alabaster feathers into the pond, which rippled gently. Jordan rested her hand on Sawyer's shoulder and he slowly reached up to cover her hand with his, his breaths growing shallower with every second. Jordan closed her eyes and lowered her head. The hopelessness in her chest was like a vice clenching her heart, and she was certain it would soon break into pieces.

Suddenly, she snapped her head up and looked at the pond again, the ripples from Victoria's tear were almost gone. "Tears!" Jordan exclaimed, and they all looked at her in confusion. Jordan jumped to her feet and stood, inches from Christian's face. "Tears made the Onirus amulet magic. It was destroyed, but you put the Nephiryon amulet in the pond. Between the amulet and the magic pond, you have to be able to save him! You saved Victoria; you can do that for Sawyer too!"

Christian's face hardened at the voiced memory of that terrible day. "I cannot," he said with a curt shake of his head. "Victoria was already a shapeshifter and was practiced in her abilities. The potion simply changed her to her alternate natural form. She was able to remain in her alternative form due to the potion. Sawyer is not a shapeshifter."

"I wasn't a shapeshifter either," Jordan pushed on persistently. "The water made me a shapeshifter because of the amulet," Jordan rushed on. "Once we put him in the water, he'll be a shapeshifter too! He'd be able to change and then you can give him the potion and he can stay that way!"

"The water will give him the ability to change, but he is far too weak to be able to learn and then accomplish it. He does not have the time nor the strength," Christian said, turning and walking to stand next to Victoria at the very edge of the pond.

Victoria's squawk broke the cool, night air. Christian looked at her and their eyes remained locked for several seconds.

"No," he said, sharply. "I will not attempt that."

"If there's anything you can try, please do it," Georgia chimed in, tears falling freely from her eyes. "Jordan deserves love. You of all people should know what this kind of loss is like! How can you let someone else suffer what you've suffered? If there's any way you can prevent it, you have to try."

The sound of Christian's knuckles cracking as he clenched his fists was audible to everyone. He turned his head to Victoria and said quickly, "We do not know the potion will work. It has not been tried in this kind of situation. And plus," his eyes shifted to Jordan, "the sacrifice would be great. And even then, nothing is guaranteed."

Jordan took another step toward Christian. "You said he's going to die anyway. If we try something, *anything*, it will only increase his chance of survival. There's nothing to lose here and everything to gain."

"On the contrary," Christian said, his voice barely audible. "There is much to lose. For you specifically, there is *everything* to lose." Jordan's look of confusion forced him to continue. "How much are you actually willing to sacrifice to save this boy?"

"Anything," Jordan said, not missing a beat. "Anything I can do to help save him I'll do. What do you need from me?"

Christian walked over to Sawyer's still body and looked down at him. "The life in him is almost gone. In order to change him, it will take blood…"

"Have it!" Jordan cried, closing the space between her and Christian again and holding out her wrist. "Take as much as you need."

"Please, let me finish," he said, gently pushing her arm back down to her side. "It will take blood directly from your heart. The freshest and strongest blood is the only way for him to have the strength he will need to come through the process and, even then, it is not guaranteed. But, if he does make it through, the combination of your heart's blood with the new potion I have developed should keep him alive in animal form for a normal magical lifetime."

Jordan stared at him for a moment before she squared her shoulders and asked, "And how will you get my heart's blood?"

Christian met her gaze and held it before answering with a single, cryptic word. "Directly."

Georgia gasped, and a wheezing sound suddenly issued from Sawyer. Jordan dropped to her knees, grabbing Sawyer's hand and putting her face close to his. "What is it?" she asked, shakily.

"No," he wheezed again, dragging in a labored breath. "You can't sacrifice yourself for me." Another ragged breath. "You have to stop Edmund."

Tears welled and spilled out of Jordan's eyes and she rested her forehead on Sawyer's, shocked at how much colder he seemed than even the winter air around them. "I won't be able to do anything if I lose you. I'm sorry." She looked up into the face of her best friend. The pain in Georgia's eyes was almost too much to bear, so she looked over to Victoria floating on the pond. "Georgia will continue this mission with one, both, or neither of us. I know she will." She looked back into Sawyer's face and grasped his hand tightly. "My life only really became worth living when you came into it and it will lose all meaning if you're gone." She kissed Sawyer's hand before placing it back on his chest and rising.

"There *may* be a way to save you both," Christian said, slowly. Jordan gasped and, without thinking, reached out and gripped the front of Christian's blood-stained shirt.

"Do it! Whatever it is, do it! If we can both be together, it would be a true miracle. If we both die, we won't know any different. And if he lives and I die, it would still be a sacrifice well worth making." She thought she saw the tiniest hint of a smile pull at the corners of Christian's mouth as he removed her hand from his shirt and knelt next to Sawyer, pulling her down with him. With his other hand, he removed a vile of luminescent yellow liquid and held it up in front of him.

"Once I have your heart's blood, I will place it in the boy's mouth along with a dose of this potion. This should complete his transformation with no effort on his part. Because we are using your blood, he will transform into the same animal which you yourself transform. If you are able to live long enough for me to complete this and make sure of his survival, I will then give the rest of the potion to you. You will still need to summon the strength to change on your own after taking the potion. Should you do this, you will also be able to live your full magical lifetime; you can live these magical lifetimes together in your animal forms.

"Yes," Jordan said, nodding vehemently. "I understand. Do it." He looked at her shrewdly and she took a deep breath before whispering, "please."

Christian looked down at Sawyer and then back into Jordan's eyes as he took a long, deep breath. His gaze never left hers as his hand reached back into his pocket and, in a flash, he pulled out a dagger and plunged it into Jordan's chest.

Chapter Twenty
A New War

Georgia's scream rang through the woods. Victoria flapped her wings in alarm.

"Stay back!" Christian yelled, his piercing look holding Georgia in her place. "If there is any chance of this working, you must not interfere!" Georgia looked to Sawyer whose eyes were closed and who laid perfectly still. He may already be dead for all she knew. Her eyes cut to Jordan who knelt, slumped toward Christian. Her eyes were wide in shock, her mouth open slightly, but she made no sound. Christian reached out to Sawyer and grabbed his shirt, dragging him closer to them with surprising strength. He squeezed Sawyer's face with his hand, forcing his mouth open slightly. He turned back to Jordan who looked at him, her teeth clenched, her hands both tightly gripping his arm that was still holding the knife in her chest. "I am going to pull this out and tend to the boy," he whispered intently. "I need you to lie still to keep what remaining strength you can and keep your heart from beating too quickly. Once I finish with him, I will be back to do your part. Do you understand?"

Jordan gave one, single nod. Christian pulled out the blade and she groaned, pinching her eyes shut tightly as he laid her gently face up on the ground, put her hand over the wound in her chest, and turned toward Sawyer. He held the knife over his open mouth and the blood dripped thickly into it. He reached for the glowing vile, uncorked it, and poured half of the liquid into Sawyer's mouth as well. He placed his hand under Sawyer's chin, forcing it closed, and tapped his throat lightly, urging him to swallow.

Nothing happened for what felt like an eternity and Georgia's shoulders began to shake with silent sobs. She sunk to her knees on the bank of the pond. She couldn't bear the thought of losing both of her friends so soon after losing her mother. Even though there were two other people in the clearing with her, people who were just like her, she felt entirely alone. These people might be like her, but they were also complete strangers. She knew some of Victoria's story, but she didn't know her really. She definitely didn't know them enough to confide in them. She didn't even know if they would associate with her after this whole ordeal was done. Just then, she felt something behind her and turned to see Victoria's head leaning gently into the small of her back.

"That's it boy, fight!" Christian's gruff words startled them both and they turned their heads to look at what was happening. Sawyer's eyes were wide open, and his body was shaking as if he were having a seizure. Christian was holding his head down with one hand, so it didn't bounce against the ground and his other was still clamped firmly on Sawyer's chin, holding his mouth shut.

"Christian?" Georgia said fearfully, rising slowly and walking toward him. "Is he ok? What…"

"The potion and the blood are doing what they are designed to do," he answered through clenched teeth. "This method of changing is more intense; traumatic. It is permanent, so his body is making more drastic changes.

But he is fighting for his life." Christian's voice held a note of admiration as he watched Sawyer struggling.

"Is there anything I can do?" Georgia asked, a note of pleading in her voice. She was having a hard time being idle while both of her friends were going through so much.

"Check on the girl," he answered. "This one is coming into the transformation. It will be her turn soon if she holds on." His words weren't intended to be hurtful, but they drilled into her heart like the knife he had just pulled from Jordan's chest. He glanced at her face and his tightened. "I am sorry. I did not mean …"

"I know," Georgia said, forgivingly. She walked over and knelt tentatively next to her best friend, looking into her face. Jordan's eyes were still squeezed shut, her jaw still clenched, one hand was squeezing the grass at her side and the other was pressed tightly over the bleeding hole in her chest. Her breathing was labored, but she *was* still breathing, and this gave Georgia hope. "Hang on, Jordan," she whispered. "Sawyer's doing great. Christian's almost done and then he's coming to you. You need to hang on. We have a lot left to finish and I… I need you," she choked back a sob and put her hand on top of Jordan's clenched hand in the grass next to her. Jordan relaxed her hand enough to turn it over and lock her fingers between Georgia's tightly. She gave another single, quick nod and remained still again.

The sound of Sawyer's yells pulled her attention away for a moment, and she raised her eyes just in time to see his body transforming from a human into a large, grey wolf's body. Christian leaned back and sat on the ground, watching as the transformation was complete. Sawyer laid still for a few moments and then slowly began to push himself up to a sitting position.

Christian rose and turned to Georgia. "Change yourself and speak to him. Ease him and tell him what is happening with this girl so he does not attack me while I work."

Georgia nodded and backed away from Jordan before transforming and walking slowly toward Sawyer. "Are you ok?" she asked tentatively. "You need to just stay sitting and try to relax while you take it all in."

"What happened to me? Where's Jordan? She didn't sacrifice herself!" his eyes found Jordan's supine body across the clearing with Christian kneeling over her and he attempted to rise and walk toward her. Georgia quickly placed herself between them, which wasn't entirely necessary as he wasn't used to walking with four legs just yet and he toppled forward onto the ground.

"Sawyer, please," she begged. "I need you to stay calm. Yes, she sacrificed herself for you, but she may be able to survive this as well. Christian's working to save her right now. You have to let him do what he needs to do."

"How can you trust him!?" Sawyer growled. "Look what he did to her!"

"Sawyer, you know she wouldn't take no for an answer," Georgia answered softly. "She loved you too much. Try to be reasonable. If she'd been the one lying there dying, and

Christian had given you the opportunity to sacrifice yourself so she could live, what would you have done?"

Sawyer lay in silence, breathing heavily. Finally, he answered quietly, "I would've done anything for her to live."

"Exactly. And he was successful with you. There was no guarantee it would work, but he brought you through this. Now, if he can bring Jordan though as well, you two will be able to be together again. It may not be how you always imagined it, but isn't it worth it to have her in your life?"

Sawyer sighed heavily. "Of course, you're right. I just can't stand seeing her lying there like that; like she's dead."

"I had to stand by and watch both of you look like that tonight," Georgia said, empathetically. "I just lost my mother. I didn't know how I was going to live if I had to lose both of you as well."

"Oh, Georgia," Sawyer got up and slowly manipulated his four limbs to walk to her. He paused next to her and leaned his shoulder against hers. "I know things have been hard on you lately. I can't imagine what that felt like. But I'm here. I'm not going anywhere."

She leaned back against him. "Thanks."

"I just hope we get to keep our girl," Sawyer said softly, his eyes still on Jordan's still legs. The rest of her was hidden behind Christian's body as he leaned over her, working on bringing around her transformation. Georgia nodded in agreement and they watched.

Christian had poured the potion into Jordan's mouth and was rubbing her throat in attempt to get her to swallow the liquid. She had lost consciousness just as he had reached her, and he was concerned she may choke if he wasn't careful about how he handled this. He put his arm under her shoulders and sat her up. He plugged her nose and waited. She opened her mouth, the potion going down her throat as she took in a breath. She coughed slightly, some of the liquid dribbling out of her mouth, but the majority of it seemed to have been swallowed. "Good girl," Christian whispered, laying her back on the ground and putting one hand on her forehead as he had done with Sawyer. Her eyes snapped opened and locked on his as her body began to vibrate.

"C-C-Christian," she said through chattering teeth.

"Shhh," he said softly, placing his other hand on her side. "This change is going to feel different. It is a permanent change. Just try to relax and push through it. It will be over soon." Her eyes closed tightly, and her body began to convulse in earnest.

"This is the worst part," Sawyer said softly, casting his eyes down to the ground, unable to watch the woman he loved suffering. "It feels like your body's being ripped apart from the inside. I felt every bone breaking, every muscle tearing and reforming." Georgia cringed at the description but couldn't pull her eyes away from the sight of her best friend.

Finally, the shaking stopped, and Jordan's scream pierced the night air as her body began to change into the wolf body Georgia had seen so often. Though the sound was terrible, the sight of the change happening lifted Georgia's spirits more than she could express. She rose to all fours. She wanted to run to her friend, but in deference to Sawyer's newness to the quadruped way of moving, she matched his pace and they walked to Jordan's side together. When they reached her, the transformation was complete and Christian stood and backed away a few steps. They all watched as she lay there, motionless.

"Why isn't she waking up?" Sawyer asked, looking at Christian.

"He can't understand you," Georgia reminded him. "We can understand him, but he can't understand us unless he's in his animal form too."

Christian, however, seemed to have either understood what Sawyer's whine had been asking, or he was wondering the same thing himself because he knelt next to Jordan's body again and shook her gently. There was still no movement. He placed his hand lightly on her throat, then looked into their concerned faces. "Her heart still beats. She was still alive when the transformation started. It is not likely she passed during the transformation; the adrenaline alone would have been enough to keep her heart beating. I am not sure why she does not wake."

"Her chest isn't rising!" Sawyer said suddenly. "She isn't breathing." He rushed forward as quickly as he could, raised up on his hind legs, and came down hard on the side wall of her furry chest. They all watched as nothing happened. Sawyer rose again and hit her chest in the same spot. A huff escaped Jordan's mouth along with a bubbling sound and another small amount of the luminescent liquid.

She sucked in a breath and opened her eyes. She found Sawyer's face and struggled to get to her feet. "What happened?" she asked, her voice hoarse. "I remember being in pain and my muscles hurting. Then everything went black."

"You apparently choked on some of the potion Christian gave you for the transformation. Sawyer just compressed it out of you." Georgia said, relieved. "We thought you didn't make it."

Jordan looked at Sawyer and her mouth twitched; the wolf equivalent of a smile. "You saved my life."

Sawyer pressed his cheek against hers and closed his eyes. He was amazed that, even in wolf form, she still smelled the same; the sweet perfume of her hair wafted into his nostrils. "Then I'd say we're even. You sacrificed yourself for me, didn't you?"

"I couldn't imagine a life worth living if you weren't in it," she whispered. "Are you mad?"

"I get to spend the rest of my life with you," Sawyer said, pulling his head back to look in her eyes. "Animal or not, that's all I want."

"I love you," they said at the same time.

Silence filled the clearing for a long while until a rustling sound near the bank of the pond drew their attention.

They all looked to see Christian had transformed back into the bear and was sitting near Victoria. "I am sorry to interrupt your moment," he said, and his sincerity was clear. "I am very happy you both made it through this and I hope you do not live to regret the decision. But there is still much to discuss, and I believe the sooner we start, the better."

Chapter Twenty-One
Aftermath

They definitely looked like a motley crew gathered around the pond; two wolves, a bobcat, a bear, and a swan. But while they were diverse, their goal was identical.

"We have to stop Edmund," Sawyer said seriously. "Everything we've gone through tonight and everything our families will have to go through because of it can't be in vain. My grandfather, Jordan's parents, Ryan, Mama Landry; so many people are going to be affected by the events of tonight. We have to stop this war; stop something like this from ever having to happen again." They all nodded in agreement.

"I have said before, if we simply drain this pond, Edmund will no longer have any way to recruit more members of his army," Victoria said, insistently.

"No!" Christian roared and they all flinched. "You had me save these two so they could be together. After all that, you must understand I cannot lose you. I will not. And even if we were to drain this pond, his numbers must be near where he needs them at this point. The damage has been done." They all hung their heads in discouragement.

It was Georgia who raised her head first. "Even if what you say is true and Edmund's numbers have increased, I may have an idea of how to keep him from bolstering those numbers." They all looked at her in silent anticipation. "If we can find where the spring leaves the pond and goes to the mill, we could block it. That way, once they use whatever water they have, they won't be able to get any more. They don't know where the spring feeding their well is. And springs dry up all the time. It may not even cause suspicion."

Christian nodded thoughtfully. "That may work," he agreed. "Victoria, are you able to do some searching and see if you can find where that spring connects to the pond?"

"I can definitely try," Victoria agreed.

"But what are we going to do about the existing soldiers?" Jordan asked, her voice losing some of its hoarseness and returning to its normal register and tone. "I may not be able to go back into town, but it is still my home and I care about the people in it. My parents are still here. They're going to be dealing with enough when I don't come back." She paused here, the thought of never seeing her parents again hitting home. She breathed deeply until she had her emotions under control. "Edmund's going to destroy them and all the people we care about if left unchecked. We can't let that happen. We can't let the evil magic spread like a cancer through this town and maybe even beyond!"

"You're right," Georgia's words were barely audible. "This is the only home I have left, and Jordan's parents are the only family I have. We have to save them and this town if we can." She looked to Jordan and Sawyer. "What am I going to tell your parents, Jordan?" Her voice broke and she paused a moment before continuing. "And Sawyer, what about your grandpa? What am I going to tell *everyone* when you both never come home again?!" Her breathing became rapid and uneven. She laid on the ground and hung her head, shaking softly with silent sobs.

Jordan and Sawyer laid down on either side of her, leaning in and nuzzling her in comfort. "Georgia, come on," Sawyer said quietly. "I know it's going to be terrible to help people believe we're gone, but we haven't really gone anywhere. You still get to see us and talk to us. You can come here any time and see us. And we'll be working together to help with the rest of this mission to keep them safe. This whole thing is so much bigger than any one of us. They may be devastated now but keeping us all alive in one form or another is our best chance to win this thing, and that will go a long way in saving them."

"Yeah, and I am relying on you to help my parents through this," Jordan added. "They love you. You're like another daughter to them. I'm not saying you should try to replace me, but your being there will definitely ease them."

"I can't bear to look at their faces when I tell them... tell them *what*?! What can I possibly tell everyone? What's going to satisfy them that you're gone and never coming back even though no bodies will ever be found?"

Everyone was quiet for a while as they thought over their options.

"You could say they simply ran away together," Victoria finally offered. "That way your parents and grandfather would not have to process your death. They would believe you left to be together."

"It's an idea, but our situation isn't the same as yours and Christian's," Jordan said. "I'd never leave my parents without talking to them about it first. And Sawyer would never have let me run away without talking to my parents."

"It's true," Sawyer agreed. "And I have a feeling your parents would never stop looking for you. I think the not knowing if you were really alive or dead would be worse than if you actually were to have died."

"It's true," Georgia nodded. "There's at least some kind of finality in death; some closure." She sighed deeply. "You're going to have to have died for them to be able to ever have a chance to move on."

The silence returned, and they continued to ponder the issue. Christian shifted a bit and they all looked to him. He huffed a sigh. "The two of you went on walks together through these woods on occasion, yes?" They nodded their assent and he continued. "I doubt you have ever gone as far as the north ridge of these woods as it is many, many miles. If you had, you would know there is a very steep cliff face about a half mile wide. It drops over one hundred feet into a river. You could have walked there on your own. Or you could have been driven there by an external force."

"I haven't ever been that far," Jordan said. "And I'm not sure what kind of force could've pushed us that far in this kind of cold weather. I mean, a forest fire could I guess. But someone would have noticed a fire big enough to push us that far north.

"I was considering a more… organic force." Even with the seriousness of the topic, there was almost a smile in Christian's voice as he offered this suggestion.

Confused silence followed this comment until Georgia let out a dry laugh. "You're thinking of the day you chased me into this clearing, aren't you?" He nodded ever so slightly, and they all sat up. "That might work. If you two went on a long walk together in that direction today and then came across a bear, you could easily get chased farther than you'd normally go. If the walk started later in the afternoon, by the time you came across the bear it could be getting dark so being chased to the cliff wouldn't be implausible. You could've burst through the tree line and not have stopped in time."

"I do not know that the details are overly important," Christian chimed in. "No one would be able to corroborate or discredit them since no one would have been there. If they fell, they would never survive the fall. The river is fairly shallow at the bottom of that cliff. The rocks would make survival next to impossible and their bodies could have been washed anywhere by the time anyone were to go looking." Georgia gave a slight shudder.

"Are you ok?" Victoria asked gently.

"I had to watch my two friends come close to dying tonight. Talking about it is a little fresh for me and knowing I have to have some really hard conversations tonight and tomorrow is really affecting me."

"Why don't you stay out here tonight?" Sawyer offered. "You can go back in the morning and tell everyone you were supposed to hear from Jordan last night after she got back from her walk with me and you didn't. You got worried, so you went out looking for her. That way you can have some time out here to collect yourself before facing everyone."

"That's tempting," Georgia said appreciatively. "But I think it'll be better to get it out of the way. I'll go to Judy and Gordon's tonight and talk to them. I'm going to need some sleep after that to recoup and they'll let me stay there, especially since we'll all be grieving. When I get up tomorrow morning, I'll go talk to Mr. Toole…"

"I don't think you're going to need to make anything up for Mr. Toole," Jordan said, thoughtfully. Georgia looked at her but didn't say anything. "We went to him for help tonight. We told him everything. He's going to know anything you make up is a lie. He'll know it had something to do with the mill. I don't know how many people we want to tell the truth about what we're doing in here, but Auggie might be someone we could trust with a bit of the information at least."

"That's true," Georgia said. "And if we tell him what happened and he *doesn't* die of heart failure, he might be a bit more forthcoming with any information he withheld until now. Plus, he's known something was up with the mill for years but never divulged anything to anyone. I think it's safe to say he's pretty trustworthy. However, in public or anyone else's company, I should tell him the cliff story. So, that just leaves Ryan for the people I'll need to tell immediately. Oh," she said, suddenly realizing something. "If you aren't working anymore, I'm probably going to have to work a lot of shifts; I mean a *lot* of them. I can't help stop this war if I'm spending all of my time at the bookstore. I won't have any time to come out here and collaborate with you!" Hysteria was creeping into her voice.

"Whoa," Jordan said, leaning hard into her friend. "Deep breaths. We should act soon on this war, but we don't need to act immediately. We'll need time to regroup, adjust to this new alliance we have going. I know it's going to be a very taxing process doing all the things you need to do with our families and in the town. The four of us will talk over things when you can't be here and fill you in whenever you can make it. Once things settle down a bit, we can start moving forward with plans to tackle Edmund's troops and put an end to the war once and for all." Georgia was quiet for a while. "Georgia?" Jordan said, tentatively.

"I don't want to do this," Georgia said, quietly but angrily. "I don't *want* to tell people you're dead. I don't *want* to go back to life in town without my friends. I don't *want* to be a part of this stupid war. I know I'm supposed to do the right thing and work to save innocent people in town from annihilation, and I'll do what I'm asked because it's the right thing to do. But it doesn't stop me from wishing... wishing I *wasn't* descendant from the Onirus family. I don't want to be magic. I don't want this life; this obligation. I never asked for this," she finished softly, a note of defeat in her voice.

Her statement lingered on the air in the quiet woods. No one knew what to say to that. They couldn't blame her for how she felt and, as the sole remaining human form that was known to everyone in town and who was able to continue moving throughout life gathering and distributing information, she would be called on for a lot of tasks.

"You are angry and bitter," Christian stated. Georgia looked at him. "It isn't a judgement," he continued quickly. "I understand why you feel that way. You are right; it is not fair you will have to do most of the foot work and communication. But the fact is, we *do* need you. You are an invaluable part of this team and this process." Georgia nodded listlessly and hung her head.

Christian looked at her intently and cleared his throat. "Georgia, you have a job to finish here; an important one. It will not be easy and a majority of it will not be enjoyable. But if you can do what we need of you and help us complete our mission, I may be able to help you with your wishes."

Everyone turned their heads to Christian in surprise. "What do you mean?" Georgia asked, skeptically.

"If you do what needs to be done and what we require of you; if you work through this war with us and fight admirably, then when this is all done, I may be able to take this burden of magic from your shoulders… permanently." He waited for a response and, when none came, he pushed on. "What do you say?"

Georgia stared at the ground thinking for a long while. She finally raised her head, her eyes blazing. "I say you've got a deal."

About the Author

J. Lawson was born in Davenport, Iowa. She went to St. Ambrose University in Davenport, Iowa for her undergrad work and Western Illinois University (QC Annex) in Moline, Illinois for her graduate studies.

Lawson moved to Peoria, Illinois in 2009. She is married to her husband, Don, and they have one son, DJ. They also have two dogs, Bailey and Loki, and one cat, Onyx.

When Lawson isn't spending her time writing, she likes to read fantasy and mystery novels, listen to 80s and 90s rock music, drink copious amounts of coffee, and discuss new book ideas with her best friend and creative consultant, Laura.

To find more information about J. Lawson visit:

twitter.com/AuthorLawson

www.facebook.com/AuthorJ.Lawson

www.AuthorJLawson.com

36649160R00144

Made in the USA
Middletown, DE
17 February 2019